REDHEADED REBELLION

Canyon O'Grady led the crowd of seething settlers to the King of Colorado's stronghold. But in their path stood a Royal Guard lieutenant with a revolver in his hand. Behind him were ten Royal Guards. They all carried Henry rifles with bayonets attached.

The lieutenant commanded the crowd, "Go back to your homes, and the King will not punish anyone for this outrage."

Now was the time for O'Grady to make his move. But as the big redhead stepped forward, the lieutenant made his.

He gave his men a quiet order and O'Grady looked into the barrels of their Henrys.

"Prepare to fire," the lieutenant snapped. "Ready, aim . . ."

CANYON O'GRADY

7

THE KING
OF
COLORADO

by

Jon Sharpe

A SIGNET BOOK

NEW AMERICAN LIBRARY

A DIVISION OF PENGUIN BOOKS USA INC., NEW YORK

SIGNET
Published by the Penguin Group
Penguin Books USA Inc., 375 Hudson Street, New York,
New York 10014, U.S.A.
Penguin Books Ltd, 27 Wrights Lane, London W8 5TZ, England
Penguin Books Australia Ltd, Ringwood, Victoria, Australia
Penguin Books Canada Ltd, 2801 John Street, Markham, Ontario,
Canada L3R 1B4
Penguin Books (N.Z.) Ltd, 182–190 Wairau Road, Auckland 10, New Zealand

Penguin Books Ltd, Registered Offices: Harmondsworth, Middlesex, England

First published by Signet, an imprint of Penguin Books USA Inc.

First Printing, May, 1990
10 9 8 7 6 5 4 3 2

 REGISTERED TRADEMARK—MARCA REGISTRADA

Printed in Canada

PUBLISHER'S NOTE
This is a work of fiction. Names, characters, places, and incidents either are
the product of the author's imagination or are used fictitiously, and any resem-
blance to actual persons, living or dead, events, or locales is entirely coinci-
dental.

Canyon O'Grady

His was a heritage of blackguards and poets, fighters and lovers, men who could draw a pistol and bed a lass with the same ease.

Freedom was a cry seared into Canyon O'Grady, justice a banner of his heart.

With the great wave of those who fled to America, the new land of hope and heartbreak, solace and savagery, he came to ride the untamed wildness of the Old West.

With a smile or a six-gun, Canyon O'Grady became a name feared by some and welcomed by others, but remembered by all . . .

*In June of 1860 Colorado was in limbo—
it was not yet a state and not yet a territory.
All sorts of men with causes and schemes
and dreams of wealth rushed into this virgin
land hoping to ride a tornado to wealth
and fortune. One of them wanted to become king,
and did . . . the King of Colorado.*

1

A rifle shot slammed through the quiet Colorado mountain air missing Shorty Balantine by six inches. He looked behind and saw five or six riders coming at him hard, all with guns out. At once Shorty did what the government man had told him to do: he jerked the horses to a stop, then jumped off the stagecoach and ran as far into the brush and tall timber as he could get.

He panted as he looked back. Six masked riders had jumped on the light celerity wagon and began tearing the rig apart. Shorty grinned when he saw the frustration on the men's faces.

He crept closer to the edge of the brush to hear them.

"What the hell? Ain't no gold on this rig," one masked man, the apparent leader, said. "And no passengers. Spread out and try to find that little driver. I got some tough questions for him."

Shorty had figured as much. He squirmed deep down in the brush, pulling branches over himself as he worked under a long-ago fallen pine tree. He had worn green and brown to make hiding easier.

The robbers hunted him for nearly half an hour, then gave up. The men had dropped their masks now with nobody to see them. The leader had a thin and mean face, hook nose, deep-set eyes, and he wore a brown hat with a hole in the crown. His skin was leathery with a slightly yellow hue. His cheeks were shrunken in and gaunt.

"Hell, we won't find him. Wid, you tie your mount to the back of this rig and get up there and drive. We can use it back in the valley for something."

They pulled out slowly and Shorty watched them go. When he was sure they were well down the road, he lifted out of the branches and walked to the rough wagon trail that led from Fort Collins to Denver.

Twenty-five yards back, Shorty saw a man ride out of the brush on a stunning palomino stallion with a pure creamy white tail and mane. He was the same man who had paid Shorty twenty dollars to drive the stage. The man rode up and nodded. "Good job, Shorty. There's a bonus for you back in Fort Collins at the Colorado Saloon. Sorry you have to walk. I've got to keep up with that rig and find out where they're taking it."

"Work for you anytime, O'Grady. Hope to see you again."

"Hope so myself," the man called O'Grady said. He rode on down the wagon road following the light, high-built wagon that substituted as a stagecoach for most companies on rough terrain routes.

Canyon O'Grady hung back a careful distance from the rig. He had to follow it but not let the highwaymen know he was there. Mostly he had to find out where they turned off. Since they decided to take the rig with them, he figured they had to be working for the King of Colorado.

Canyon rode tall in the saddle; his alert eyes saw every movement in the woods and kept a close watch on the tracks below him. His keen hearing let him ride just out of sight of the creaking celerity wagon ahead of him. He wasn't sure what he would be riding into. This new assignment, which had come directly from the President of the United States, involved mail theft, kidnapping, and insurrection. That is, if he could believe all the reports he had read over the past few days.

Ahead, the wagon had come to a stop on the trail

between Fort Collins and Denver. The area hadn't quite met all the qualifications yet to be a territory, but the politicians said Colorado should conform within the next year.

The wagon sat there as O'Grady edged forward through light timber just off the trail to determine what the stage robbers were doing. It was soon apparent. Two of the riders had tied ropes on the end of a two-foot-thick pine log along side the trail. Their horses strained and pulled the small end of the log to one side.

As soon as the log was moved, the driver guided the rig past it and into a faint trail that led to the right. When the rig was into the trees past the log, the same two riders reversed their pull and dragged the log back into position. Then they brushed out the marks, scattered fresh leaves and small branches, and returned the area to what looked like a natural state. They wiped out the tracks of the celerity wagon with pine branches back twenty yards on the main road, then brushed out their own tracks as they headed into the brush and ran back to their horses. The men mounted, made sure the side trail could not be noticed, then rode forward to catch up with the wagon.

So that was why he hadn't been able to find any trails leading off to the right when he traveled this road twice in the past few days, O'Grady decided. He touched his heels to the palomino and the horse moved forward.

"Come on Cormac, lad, we have the scent now. We'll find this King of Colorado and turn him into a peasant."

Canyon moved up closer now so he wouldn't lose the wagon. He kept back just enough so he could watch for any kind of guards or lookouts along the trail that they might tip him off to as they passed.

The first one came less than three miles in from the main trail. The wagon had rounded a small bend in

11

the faint road when the rig and its escort stopped, a log across the lane blocking it effectively.

Two of the men tied ropes to the log as before and used their horses to drag the small end of the pine log out of the way so the rig could pass.

"Wondered when you'd be back," a voice called from high on the slope to the left. Canyon peered through trees, moved a little, and then saw a man maybe a hundred feet up the side of a canyon waving with his rifle.

Guard Number One. Canyon figured there would be at least three along the way. Perhaps more at the other end of the trail if everything he had heard about the King of Colorado was true. So far it looked much as the reports had told him.

The reports. There were always reports. This time he had been in Washington and the president asked to see him personally. Often his assignments came from some top-level army staff officer with stars on his shoulder. This time President James Buchanan himself had ordered Canyon front and center.

O'Grady had been inside the Executive Mansion several times by now, but it was always a thrill to walk up past the four great white pillars fronting the building and be allowed inside. Always an army officer went with him as far as the president's private office door.

The big Oval Room was richly furnished with a plush carpet on the floor, a huge cherry-wood desk polished to a high sheen, and an inlaid writing table on the other side. A large unfurled United States flag stood in one corner and one with the great seal of the presidency stood in the other.

The president wore a stiff white collar over his white shirt fronted with a winged tie, a black frock coat, and afternoon trousers. President Buchanan stood and held out his hand as O'Grady was announced.

"Ah, yes, our knight-errant. It's good to see you again, Canyon O'Grady."

"Thank you, sir, it's good to be back."

The president motioned to a chair and O'Grady sat down. Buchanan watched his agent through his penetrating blue eyes. The president's pure white hair tufted sharply just above his forehead. That and the usual habit of cocking his head to one side were said by some to diminish his authority.

Canyon O'Grady had no such thoughts. The weight of President Buchanan's personality and the tremendous power of his office came through unfettered to O'Grady.

"What can I do for you, Mr. President?"

"You may remember that my father came from Ireland, just as yours did. So I'm thinking maybe we can double up on the luck of the Irish to get a small matter settled. Mr. O'Grady, have you ever heard of the King of Colorado?"

"The king . . . No, sir, I'm afraid not."

"Good, good. The fewer people who do hear of him, the better. You'll get a complete report of everything we know about him. Briefly, he's an ex-army colonel with an exemplary record right up to the end. Then he went a little out of his mind and was retired."

The president frowned and continued, "That was seven years ago. Now he turns up in the northeast section of Colorado, where evidently he's barricaded himself in some mountain valley and runs it like his own little kingdom. He even calls himself the King of Colorado."

"And the army, sir?"

"As you know, our army is tied up right now with Indians and this other matter we may be facing shortly, secession. Fact is we did send in a detachment, a fifteen-man scouting patrol with two officers. Only one man came back. He said he had played dead for two days before he could crawl away. The rest of the detail was slaughtered by superior numbers.

"Our main problem is the U.S. mail. We're proud

of our ability to transport letters and mail across every state and territory in the union, and some areas not quite territories yet. This man's henchmen have attacked three stage coaches carrying U.S. mail, captured the coaches and all their passengers, and neither the people nor the mail has been seen since.''

''Yes sir, I see.''

''We have reports of other people missing in the area. The most recent event was another stage. The company had sent armed guards along. Two of the three guards were gunned down and the coach, the people, and the horses were all driven off somewhere; nothing has been heard of them since.

''I want you to go out there, O'Grady, work your way into that damned 'kingdom,' find out what's going on, and put a stop to it.''

''Yes, sir.''

The president got up and walked to one of the windows and looked out on the lawn and trees. ''I have reports that of our six U.S. agents, you're the top man.''

''I do my best, Mr. President,'' Canyon said.

''They say you can think or fight your way out of the toughest situation. This might be one of those. I don't want to send in an army regiment. I'm looking to have this situation cleaned up and this king fellow dethroned as quickly as possible.''

''I understand, Mr. President.''

''Now, Mr. O'Grady. I can provide you with experts from the army, fighters, scouts, heliograph men, transportation, expense money, whatever you need.''

''Sir, this sounds like something I need to work alone on. I'll have to infiltrate into the area, scout it out, and figure how to dethrone this person.''

''Good. If indeed you decide you'll need a company or two of infantry, you come out and you'll get the troops. But we just can't send in men blind, not knowing what they'll face.''

"Agreed, sir. I'd expect you want this done as soon as possible, Mr. President?"

The tall, white-topped President of the United States nodded and O'Grady shook his hand and left. On his way out, the army colonel who escorted him handed Canyon a packet of material in a brown envelope.

"This matter is confidential, Mr. O'Grady. When you have read it and won't need it anymore, your instructions are to burn it and stir the ashes. Understood?"

Now, staring at one of the King of Colorado's sentries who controlled the entryway through this small gorge, O'Grady had a better feel for his mission. The orders had been specific: to investigate and put an end to the King of Colorado. Sounded easy, but it was looking more complicated all the time.

O'Grady surveyed the possibilities: he could wait for darkness and slip through undetected, but then he would lose the stolen wagon and miss finding other checkpoints and lookouts.

He eased Cormac sharply to the left and worked silently through the trees and up the gentle slope of the far side of the ravine. The sentry had been about a hundred feet up on a small ledge.

After five minutes of cautious movement, Cormac had brought Canyon to a level part of the slope. The cover gave way ahead, and O'Grady knew he would have to work on foot from now on. He slid from the big palomino, patted his neck, and tied him to a tree limb.

The U.S. agent moved carefully through the light brush and an occasional black oak. It took him nearly ten minutes to walk and crawl forty yards to a point where he could see the sentry.

The man had carved out a comfortable yet concealed lookout spot by cutting brush to a small clearing, making a stool from an upturned log, and generally setting up a good little camp. He had a sleeping area, a place for a small cooking fire, and a supply of food and three blankets. He was a permanent lookout and might not be missed for three or four days.

O'Grady inched forward and crouched behind the white blossoms of a mountain mahogany bush that stood eight feet tall. He peered around: the King's sentry was staring the other way at a redheaded woodpecker who was drilling a hole in a piñon's bark where he would deposit an acorn.

Canyon lifted to his feet and walked silently the last three yards, his six-inch-bladed hunting knife out and ready. When he was four feet from the guard, the man must have sensed danger. He whirled, trying to draw his six-gun from hip leather at the same time. The free-swinging holster flared outward, spoiling the man's grab, and by then O'Grady's knife lay against the sentry's throat and he had the man's left hand twisted behind his back.

The guard swung his free right hand at the knife. His hand hit Canyon's unprotected wrist. The movement powered O'Grady's arm and hand downward, causing the blade to slice deeply through soft throat tissue and the left carotid artery. Blood, suddenly freed from the high pressure of the pumping heart, surged outward in regular beats and spurted into the air.

The sentry tried to scream but only gurgles and a froth of blood came out. His eyes turned to see his killer and then went blank.

O'Grady dropped the dead man on the ground. With so much blood around, it would be impossible to fake a defection by the guard. Canyon quickly slid some of the food supply into his small backpack and hurried back to Cormac. He had to catch up with the wagon in case there were more checkpoints.

2

As Canyon rode down the faint trail at a canter to catch up to the wagon, he thought over the background material he had read on Colonel Jacob B. Klingman, now the self-styled King of Colorado. The colonel had graduated from West Point and served in various units and commands; he performed well against the Indians and was promoted steadily.

Reports stated he was ticketed for his first star in minimum time. Then he had a fateful fight with a hundred Comanches deep in Texas. The colonel was seriously wounded, lost half of his command, most of his confidence, and, reports indicated, all of his sanity. He was never the same after that fight. He was sent to Omaha for observation, then to Philadelphia, and at last discharged with full retirement pay and privileges.

Colonel Klingman dropped out of sight for two years, then five years ago he showed up in Fort Collins in the Colorado area, talking of a special colony where everyone worked to help everyone else. It would be a paradise. He quickly gained a following. They pooled their money and possessions and bought supplies to start a self-sustained colony in the middle of the mountains. That spring they left Fort Collins and vanished into the vast unexplored and unsettled Rocky Mountains.

From time to time a wagon would come out to buy certain essentials they couldn't produce and didn't want to go without: salt, sugar, ax heads, saw blades, and the like. But the driver wouldn't say where they were, and no one ever followed the wagon or tracked it. Nobody was that interested.

Then for a year no one saw any of the people from the colony. Soon came reports of travelers along some of the nearby trails vanishing without a trace.

Rumors slipped out that there was a "King of Colorado" who had his kingdom not far from Fort Collins, but nobody knew exactly where it was. There was talk that the king was the former Colonel Klingman who had left Fort Collins some years before.

The colonel had taken a wife and teenage daughter with him into his paradise. Tales of gold came out, but no one could ever find it. The rumors said that the King of Colorado mined a huge area in the high mountains and forced all prospectors out or killed them. Twice now a herd of cattle had appeared on the trail heading for Denver. Some said the cattle were from the ranches owned by the King of Colorado.

Nobody knew for sure.

People in Fort Collins figured the king had to have someone living in the town, a spy who reported to him regularly. But again, no one really knew.

When the first stages began running from the village to Denver, the third one through carried a large sum of cash for the new Fort Collins bank. The shipment was secret, but the stage was robbed and the perpetrators vanished into the woods. Everyone in the area figured the King of Colorado was behind it.

Now the stories coming out from the Klingman colony changed. It was no longer a paradise. Those who wanted to leave were not permitted. You could come into the kingdom, but no one could go back out.

In the past six months the attacks on the stagecoaches were stepped up. Most often the coach, passengers, drivers, and the horses were all taken

18

somewhere—it was whispered into the kingdom of the King of Colorado.

Canyon O'Grady had arrived in Fort Collins with no one knowing who he was or why he was there. He had said he was looking for a spot to start a small business. That let him talk to half the people in Fort Collins. Then he talked to the stage-company people and told them in confidence why he was really in town and what he wanted to do. They agreed to cooperate.

For a week he circulated rumors that a large gold shipment was coming from a mine in the Fort Collins area and would be sent directly to the new federal mint in Denver on a secret stage. He made it sound good. There would be two hundred thousand dollars in gold on the stage.

O'Grady had arranged for several wooden boxes to be built, and at night he had loaded them with sand. The next morning they went on the special coach of the Fort Collins–Denver Stage Company. Shorty was hired to drive the rig. O'Grady told him exactly what to expect and what he should do the moment he heard the first shot or saw a group bearing down on him. Then they set out, O'Grady riding Cormac behind and just in sight of the stage as a rear observer.

He figured the king would pounce on the gold like a swallow attacking a nest-robbing crow.

The king certainly did.

Canyon O'Grady pulled himself back to the present and realized that he could hear the team ahead and the shouts and calls of some men. They must be near another checkpoint, he thought. O'Grady rode up in the brush off the trail and soon saw a small log cabin up ahead. A stiff hog wire fence eight feet high stretched across the trail, with a sturdy log gate shutting off access.

Three men came out of the log cabin and talked and joked with the raiding party. The gate swung open and the celerity wagon drove through. There was more talk, then the log gate closed, was locked in place, and the three men at the outpost drifted back inside their cabin.

The gate was at a narrow part of a tiny valley they had been working up. There was no way through it.

But there might be one around it.

Canyon found that the wire stretched deep into the brush on each side of the small valley to a point where not even Cormac could get around it. He looked at the height of the log gate, little more than four feet. Cormac had jumped higher fences.

It took Canyon a few minutes to find the dry materials he wanted and to get a fire burning well against the back side of the cabin. By the time the smoke drifted in the down-wind window of the cabin, O'Grady was back astride Cormac in the closest brush to the cabin.

In moments the three men ran out, saw the fire, and quickly got buckets and raced away for water to douse the flames.

As soon as all three scampered out of sight for the stream, O'Grady worked Cormac out of the brush and trotted soundlessly on the soft footing to within twenty feet of the gate. Then the government agent kicked Cormac in the flanks and pointed him at the gate. The big stallion took half a dozen galloping strides toward the fence, lifted up and over it without even a hoof ticking the top rail. The big stallion came down and quickly rushed around the bend in the trail and out of sight.

By the time the men had the blaze put out, they swore at the raiders who had just come through. Those devils had set the fire as a prank, wondering how long it would take the guards to find it.

Canyon didn't wait to see what the guards did. He took the next mile at a lope and quickly caught up with the slow-moving celerity wagon over the rough trail.

By now he estimated that they were more than seven miles from the Denver road. The small valley opened into a larger one between high peaks that must have gone up to twelve thousand feet. Even in June they all had snow on them. The trail became better and O'Grady and the wagon made good time for a while. There was always enough concealment along the trail or beside it, so O'Grady could keep within sight of the wagon without the escort spotting him.

By sundown, they had moved at least fifteen miles from the Denver road, Canyon estimated. They still worked through low passes and from one small valley to the next, riding almost due west into the higher peaks.

It was almost dark when the raiders settled into a camp near one of the several streams they had followed. O'Grady watched with a small pang of envy as they lit a fire and warmed themselves around it as they cooked food. With darkness the air grew chilly. Canyon went back a quarter of a mile and picketed Cormac and had a cold meal from the food he had snatched from the kingdom's lookout.

He had no trouble sleeping. If anything came within a hundred yards of Cormac larger than a jackrabbit, he would let O'Grady know about it.

Canyon was up before dawn, fed the big animal a pound of oats, and let him drink his fill, then moved out to find the celerity wagon. It was where he had left it. The raiders slept late. They got up about eight and had a cooked breakfast, then continued on.

O'Grady followed the raiders through one more lush valley, where he saw a large herd of cattle grazing. Then they climbed over a low pass, and on top of it they came to another checkpoint. It also had a counterbalanced wooden gate, which quickly swung aside for the wagon and escort. On both sides of the gate there were fences made of four strands of smooth wire nailed to sturdy posts.

But unlike the other one, this fence ran only slightly into the timber of juniper, piñon pine, and a sprinkling of ponderosa pine and blue spruce. O'Grady had no trouble working Cormac through the trees around the fence and down to the trail on the far side.

Now the trail had become a well-traveled road, with wagon tracks and horseshoe prints. Canyon began to see more people as the trail wound down the far side of the pass into a broad valley he guessed might be ten miles long. It was a hidden valley and he saw why the colonel wanted to start a colony here. It was like a paradise. Plenty of water in the summer, but it would have a bitter cold winter.

Fort Collins had an elevation of almost five thousand feet, and Canyon had been climbing at least half the time since he left the Denver road. They must be seven thousand feet in the air, O'Grady thought. He estimated that they had traveled at least twenty-four miles from the Denver road. He was really in the back woods.

Even so, he saw more and more people. Here and there he found men cutting logs and hauling them downhill. Once on the valley floor, he found considerable cultivation of the land near the streams. Occasionally he saw a rough log house around a cultivated area. Concealment for him was becoming difficult and nearly impossible.

He had to let the celerity wagon move on ahead. It would be going to the castle or headquarters or village, whatever the king had built for himself.

Canyon knew he couldn't simply walk in and dethrone the king. What he needed was more information. Was there really a king? Were the people not permitted to come and go as they pleased? He had a hundred other questions.

The government agent moved off the road down a lane toward a house and barn a mile into the valley. When he came into the yard six men and four women hurried out of the house and lined up in smart military fashion. The tallest of the men saluted.

O'Grady lifted a hand in a semblance of a salute.

"Farm Twenty-three, sir. We raise mostly dry beans. There are three families here at Twenty-three. What can we do for you this morning, sir?"

"Get the others about their work. I'd like to talk to you alone," Canyon said.

The man nodded, flicked out his hand, and the others scattered some to the barn, two women to the house, a third woman to a garden.

"Inside," Canyon said, wondering at the show of disciplined fear that he had seen. The king must have iron-bound control over these people. Anyone on a horse was probably a supervisor or an officer of some kind, he thought. He dismounted, tied Cormac to a post, and followed the man into the house.

It was of new log construction, but utilitarian, with bunks stacked four high along one wall. There was a cooking area, a table made of smooth split logs with benches, and a fireplace for cooking and another for warming.

The farmer, wearing faded blue pants and a brown shirt, motioned O'Grady to the table. A woman quickly brought mugs of hot coffee and freshly baked rolls.

"How long have you been in our valley?" O'Grady asked.

"Only six months. I'm one of the stagecoach people, and not to be trusted, sir." There was a bite, a lot of anger in the words.

"But you are loyal to our king?"

"Of course. What other course is there?"

"Isn't it dangerous for you to be talking to a stranger this way?"

"I'm well-known for my loyal opposition to the king," the man snapped. "We are all prisoners here,

23

we are . . ." He stopped himself, fear bathing his features.

Canyon grinned. "You might be just the man I'm looking for. I just rode in from the wagon road following a stage captured yesterday. I'm trying to find out what's going on in here."

The man's jaw dropped. "You actually broke into this place? Dozens wish they could break out of it. I'm trapped here with my wife and daughter; we were all on a stage going to Denver."

"Let's see what you can tell me, and perhaps everyone can do as he pleases in a week or so. I need all the information you know about the king and his control over the people."

The man trembled with anticipation. "It's almost too much to hope for. We've been prisoners here for over six months. I'll try to tell you everything. First, we're all slaves—royal subjects, at the call of the king or his slave masters. He calls them supervisors. I've heard he's a crazy ex-army colonel. Is that right?"

"Yes. How does he control the people? How many of you are there here? Where is his castle, his headquarters? Does he have lots of guns?"

The man put down his coffeecup and held out his hand. "Now I believe who you are. My name is David Cuzick. I'm in this country only a few years. I will help you with my life. First thing we must do is hide your magnificent horse."

The agent took his hand. "I'm Canyon O'Grady and I'm working with people who want to bring this kingdom back into what will soon be the Territory of Colorado and free everyone."

"Hallelujah to that! But in here horses are wealth and power among the leaders. Any supervisor who sees this beast will take it. His lieutenant will then take the horse from the supervisor and so on until the colonel himself, the deadly one, will be riding him and they will be hunting you."

"Hide him. His name is Cormac. Keep him safe."

Cuzick went to the door, shouted, and a moment later talked with a young boy of about twelve. The boy ran off, untied Cormac, patted his neck and talked with him a moment, and then led him toward a small feeder creek deeper into the valley.

Cuzick stepped back into the cabin. "Now, my new friend, O'Grady. What can I tell you and how can I help you overthrow the king?"

They talked for an hour, then one of the men ran to the house and whispered to Cuzick. The man left.

"Our real supervisor is coming. We must hide you."

One of the women Canyon had seen before hurried up from one of the other rooms.

"Pa, hide him in our bedroom. Not even Waldron would barge into the women's bedroom."

Cuzick pondered it a moment. "Yes, take him with you. Hide him and be careful. Waldron is not a fool."

"Yes, Pa." She caught O'Grady's hand and pulled him along. "Hurry, we don't have much time."

One room opened off a door, and inside, he saw three beds on the floor. To one side was a closet with wire hangers on a broomstick. The walls were the raw logs unfinished, some with small branch stubs on them.

The girl stopped. She was short and a little heavy. "I'm Ella," she said. She had black eyes, a pretty smile, and breasts that bounced as she walked.

"I'm Canyon O'Grady," he replied.

"You'll have to do exactly what I tell you for the safety of all of us. If Waldron catches you here, we'll all be publicly flogged and I'll have to walk through the village naked with everyone watching."

"What should I do?"

"First we wait to see what Waldron does. If he comes in here, I'll be half-undressed and you'll be under the bed. You have a revolver. All firearms are

25

illegal for us common folks. Not even the supervisors can carry a revolver. They use clubs instead.''

They heard something in the other room and looked through a small crack where Ella held the door open. O'Grady saw a man standing at the open door of the cabin.

The figure marched inside and looked around. ''All right, Cuzick, you rebellious devil. I've had reports of a horseback rider in this area. Nobody out here is supposed to have a farm horse, and I know damn well my captain ain't out here.'' He smacked his sturdy two-foot-long club into his open palm. ''I'm gonna take this place apart log by log until I find the bastard rider, and by tonight I'll be a goddamned lieutenant.''

Waldron growled and raised the club above Cuzick.

3

"Back up, you bastard," Waldron said, swinging the club as he advanced. "If I find anybody here, you are one dead farmerman, you hear me?"

"There's nobody here, I told you that once. You're slowing down my work. How can I get my work done if you keep nosing around the place?"

"Shut up and sit down."

Waldron knew how to search a cabin, especially one with as few places to hide in as this one. He checked in the large cupboards, in the bunks, in the storage place overhead. Then he went toward the two back rooms.

"Those are private rooms," Cuzick said.

"That's why I'm looking in them." He rammed open one door so it hit the wall on the other side, stormed in the bedroom, and checked under the bed and inside closets. Nothing.

He went to the second room.

"That's the women's bedroom," Cuzick said sharply. "You remember the trouble you got in last time."

"Maybe it was worth it," Waldron snorted. He pushed in the door.

Ella sat on her bed and turned around, as if startled. She was half-undressed, bare to the waist, her bare breasts swaying and bouncing. She held her chemise in one hand.

"You again, Waldron. Don't you ever knock?" She

turned her bare back to him and slipped on the under-garment and then a blouse.

"I yelled that I was dressing," Ella spat.

"Maybe I didn't hear you," Waldron said, watching her. "Damn, you still got great-looking knockers there, girl."

"That's what got you in trouble before, remember? Now get out of my bedroom or I'll complain directly to Lieutenant Johnson."

"Damn but you are a feisty one. Have to tame you yet."

"You couldn't tame a pussy cat. Now get the hell out of here!" Ella stood, in her anger evidently forgetting she hadn't put on her skirt yet. It fell to the floor, revealing her crotch and a triangle of soft brown fur. She saw her skirt drop, muttered something, and turned at once.

Waldron laughed. "Yeah, you're a show-off, that's what you are, Ella. But I'm not letting your teasing get me in trouble this time. I'll catch you alone one of these days . . ." He turned, slammed shut the door, and waved the club again in front of Cuzick.

"Quite a little girl you got there, Cuzick. Yeah! Now, maybe that stranger didn't come this way. But I'll take a damn good look around. If I find him or that gold horse, you're gonna be standing on tiptoes mouth-deep in shit." Waldron continued on out the door, slapping the heavy stick in his hand. "Damn, when will you people ever learn," Waldron said. "You do things the king's way or you don't do them at all."

In the women's bedroom, Canyon O'Grady pulled up from where he had hidden under the bed, and chuckled. "Ella, you put on quite a show for the supervisor. I'd say he was about half a step away from dropping his drawers and raping you."

"He's tried before," Ella said her back to O'Grady. "I kicked him right in his nuts the last time, and he

28

remembers it. He still wants me." Ella turned around and lifted her chemise and blouse to show her full, heavy breasts, with large pink areolas and thumb-size bright-pink nipples.

"I could put a chair under the doorknob right now," Ella said. She lifted quickly to her knees on the bed and showed him she was naked down below.

"Sweet lady, you did enough for me already. Not that I don't admire the delicious scenery. Maybe later? I got to talk more with your pa."

Ella shrugged. "Just asking. We couldn't right now anyway, not with Pa here. Later, yeah, tonight. I'll find you."

She slid into her clothes and O'Grady moved to the door, peered out through a crack, then went into the main room.

Cuzick came in from outside.

"Mr. Cuzick, I can't stay here. I didn't know I was putting you and your family in such mortal danger. I'll find a place down on the creek and camp out. But we do need to talk more."

"Right, we'll talk. First I want to check to be sure Waldron keeps moving. He's a sneaky bastard sometimes." Cuzick went out the front door and sat on the porch on a bench and watched the King's man walking down the lane toward the main road.

"He usually spends most of his time in the village. It's three miles straight north of here near the castle. Oh, yes, our King has a castle. Made out of logs, but it's a damn fine castle. Five men got killed building it. They were hoisting those big logs up for the beamed ceiling and a chain broke."

Cuzick signaled one of his farmhands and the man wandered down the way Waldron had gone. The hand was cutting weeds and checking on the growth of the beans in long rows in the field.

"Lenny will make sure Waldron keeps going back

29

to town for at least another two miles. If Waldron gets that far, he won't double back. We know Waldron."

"He has a certain area to patrol?"

"Depends. They change around a lot so we can't rely on anything. The colonel really knows what he's doing."

"You mean the king?"

"No, Colonel Shooter Daniel. He's in charge of security and defense for the King."

"A man I'll want to meet one of these days," Canyon said.

"You'll get a chance to see him tonight. There's a public punishment session. Everyone in the whole valley has to be there to witness it."

"Like in medieval times."

"About the same, except most of us know it shouldn't be this way. We're not serfs or peasants here, we're prisoners."

"How many of you prisoners are there in the kingdom?"

"Hard to say. I'd guess maybe three hundred. Klingman took converts and volunteers for three years, then shut it off and wouldn't let anybody leave. They had it good in the first years, a commune-type existence. Then the colonel went real crazy and put up his checkpoints and roadblocks and started hanging anyone who tried to run out. They say he hung twenty men in two weeks."

"Couldn't three hundred people do something about it?"

"How? He had all the guns. No one was allowed a gun in the old days, and now it's a hanging offense. The people have only pitchforks, axes, and clubs against Henry rifles that will shoot all day without reloading."

"Then we won't do it by force. We'll have to work out a better plan. That's what I'm here for."

"One man can't do much, O'Grady. Even a big one like you."

They talked most of the rest of the afternoon. Cuzick's wife let out one of her husband's plain blue shirts so it would fit Canyon. She lengthened a pair of his old pants as well, so O'Grady could go to the public punishment tonight and not show up as a stranger.

Mrs. Cuzick hid Canyon's six-gun and Henry rifle deep in the woods wrapped in oilcloth to keep them dry and safe. Her hands had trembled when she wrapped them. She showed him where they were so he could get them if he needed them.

That evening they had soup and brown bread from wheat they grew themselves.

"We eat better than ninety percent of the people because we can raise most of our own food," Ella said. She sat beside O'Grady at the table. It was a small table, and crowded, and her hand kept straying under the table, onto his leg. He moved her eager fingers back twice, then she grabbed his hand and pulled it between her open legs. Her hand shot to his crotch and rubbed.

Canyon's fingers probed and worked forward until he felt soft cotton and a small damp spot. He stroked it half a dozen times, then came away. Ella had two of the buttons on his fly opened. He brushed her hand away, quickly secured the buttons, and stood.

"I better go check on Cormac before our walk to town. Lester, that was your name, wasn't it?"

The brown-eyed twelve-year-old boy nodded. "I'll show you where he is. That's a mighty fine horse, but we got to keep him hid real good."

At the creek, O'Grady unsaddled the mount, fed him a ration of oats, and let him drink all he wanted. Then he put him on a ten-foot line so he could get to the water if he wanted to. He patted the big stallion's neck. "You hang tough here for a couple of days. I'm going to need you later on."

Canyon, Cuzick, and Ella walked together toward the village. The walk was an eye-opener for O'Grady. The community showed a lot of sense, with some cleverly worked-out uses of the land, irrigation, and crops.

"Most of the good things here happened before the king took over as all-powerful ruler," Cuzick said. "I hear it was a thriving place before that. They produced most of the things they needed and were about to start a stage line through to Loveland and Fort Collins, the two little towns out on the main road. The King stopped all of that and forced the people to produce surplus to arm and feed his army."

"Tell me about this army," Canyon said. "How many men does he have? What type of weapons?"

"Nobody knows how many men he has. I figured there are not more than about one hundred eighty men in the whole valley. The rest are women and kids. I've never seen more than twenty of his Royal Guards at a time. They have fancy uniforms with red hats and jackets and green pants."

"They all carry Henry rifles?"

"Yes, with bayonets fixed, usually."

They passed a few other farming areas, then came nearer to the village and more homes. Soon there were neat streets with identical log houses set back in regimented rows. A few blocks on, they came to stores and shops where craftsmen worked.

A block past this complex and toward the side of the hill, they came to the meeting square. A big meeting hall sat to the right side; it looked like it could hold about two hundred people. The square held a few benches, but most of the people stood around the sides. At the head of the square stood a throne of some kind of rich hardwood, carved and polished to a gloss.

Above the throne area stood the palace. It was a four-story log structure, with surging lines and open spaces that made it look like a real castle. It was all made of peeled logs that had been coated with linseed oil or some such dressing to help preserve the outside sections.

A trumpet sounded a fanfare and the square grew silent. The palace door opened on the ground floor and a man swept out; he was surrounded by the twenty Royal Guards. Each man had a Henry rifle with bayonet attached. They headed down the grassy slope to the throne. Directly behind the honor guard walked a woman alone, wearing pure white robes with a train twenty feet long.

"The Queen?" Canyon whispered.

Ella shook her head. "She's his daughter, Princess Melissa. The queen died a year ago and they had six months of mourning."

A few persons looked sharply at Ella. She scowled back at them, but she kept quiet.

The king came to the throne and seated himself. His daughter walked up and stood at his right hand. Another blast of the trumpet from somewhere on one of the castle balconies, and three people were marched in from the side. Their guards wore green uniform jackets and pants, and each carried a black club with a leather band.

Two of the prisoners were men, one was a woman.

"Begin," the king boomed in a stentorian voice.

One of the guards with a red cap and jacket roughly jerked the woman to the front of the crowd and stood her on a green square of grass in front of the king. With his knife the guard slowly cut the woman's clothes from her until she was naked. None of the three prisoners had been allowed shoes.

The man with the red hat slowly turned the woman around. She was in her thirties, slightly fat, with small breasts, and now totally humiliated. Two of the guards ran forward and each took hold of one of her arms and they paraded her down one aisle and back up the other through the crowd of punishment-watchers. They would do so until the public punishment was over.

When that began, the man with the red hat and jacket turned to the two men. "Strip them to the waist," he bellowed.

"He's Colonel Daniel," Ella whispered of the man giving the orders.

The men's shirts were pulled off and thrown on the ground, then each man was tied to one of the sturdy wooden poles that had been sunk in the ground some time before. The men's hands were thrust through large round rings on each side of the post, then their hands tied behind the post.

"For the crime of disrespect to a supervisor and threatening a supervisor with great bodily harm . . . ten lashes." Colonel Daniel barked out the sentence with a strong, sure voice.

He looked at the other man. "For the crime of disrespect to a security lieutenant and talk of and plotting to escape . . . twenty lashes."

A murmur of surprise and anger flooded through the crowd, but it was cut off abruptly when the Colonel shouted for silence. "Let the punishment begin," he cried.

Two masked men dressed all in black leather came from the sides of the crowd. Both carried short cat-o'-nine-tails with sturdy leather-covered handles.

"Twenty," Ella whispered. "The man will die. Nobody has lived through more than fifteen."

"Begin," the Colonel shouted. The leather men began their duty. When the first slash of the raw strips of leather simultaneously thundered down on the two men's bare backs, both screamed. Nine red welts popped out on the pale skin on each man. Again the leathers descended, and this time one man began screaming and sobbing.

On the fifth stroke, the man to get ten fainted. The man with twenty due had stopped screaming. He was praying. Then he began shouting loudly every evil and foul thing he could say about the king. His words rang out loud, and all could hear.

The king had been unconcerned at first; now he heard the words. He reached in his robes and pulled out a long-barreled revolver. He bellowed a command and the whipper ceased and stood back. It took the king four shots to kill the man. His second shot struck a ten-year-old-boy in the front row, injuring him. The wounded boy was not allowed to be carried off until they all were dismissed.

The king's face flushed now from the anger. He tossed his revolver to one of the guards, turned quickly, and marched up the green lawn back toward the palace.

O'Grady was too far back to see the expression of the princess clearly, but he could tell she was troubled. She had winced with each lash of the whip. Then, when the shooting began, she turned her head away but stayed in place. When her father turned toward the castle, she ran in front of him, her long train flowing behind her, lifting off the ground. At the castle door she took one last look behind her, then she rushed into the castle and Canyon thought she had burst into tears just as she entered the building.

The King of Colorado was insane, but there might be hope for his daughter, the beautiful Princess Melissa.

4

The colonel watched the king walk safely into his castle, then blew a whistle and the royal subjects scattered slowly away from the square, murmuring angrily. The king himself had never before shot a man in public punishment that way.

"The king has indeed lost his mind," one man mumbled near Cuzick.

The farmer looked up and shushed him. "Not so loud, friend. Not so loud. We don't want to see you on the whipping post next time."

Soon most of the people turned into their streets or houses and only four groups walked slowly toward the fields.

Cuzick came alongside Canyon, who had blended in with the other people well enough to go unnoticed. Now it was nearing dusk and everyone felt safer.

"O'Grady, you've just seen the basic discipline of the valley," Cuzick said. "Talk back to your supervisor and it's five lashes. A man can take a year to get over a whipping like that."

"I can appreciate the situation. I don't want to put you and your family and friends in danger. I'll sleep in the brush along the creek tonight and watch for Waldron in the morning. I have much more to learn. Where are the weapons kept? Where is the powder magazine? How many men can the colonel gather together if he has to?"

"We can talk more. There are a few of us who will

gladly help you in any attempt to overthrow the king. A pitchfork is far better than a rifle bayonet at close quarters.''

Back at the cabin, Cuzick and O'Grady talked for an hour in the dim front room. Lights would only cause suspicion. Ella brought them coffee and then went to bed.

Canyon took in all of the information about the defenses Cuzick had heard about, which was little, then the agent yawned and held out his hand. ''Cuzick, I appreciate your help. I'll be gone tomorrow on a reconnaissance, but I'll be back. Don't worry about me unless you see me tied to that whipping post.''

They shook hands and O'Grady slipped out the door and headed for the creek. He had gone less than twenty yards when he heard someone behind him. He whirled only to see Ella running toward him. She held out her arms and he caught her and swung her off her feet.

Her mouth closed over his in a passionate kiss that ended only when she wanted it to.

''Been wanting to do that half the day, Canyon O'Grady. Come on, I've got a fine little bed fixed for the two of us down by the creek.''

He looked at her. ''Won't your mother know?''

''Of course.'' She kissed him again, her tongue darting into his open mouth. ''It was Mother's suggestion. Mother says the best way for a girl to get married is to get pregnant, then pick out one of the man she bedded who she likes the most and tell him he was the only one. Works damn near every time.''

''That's not fair,'' O'Grady said.

''It isn't, but it works.'' Ella laughed there in the moonlight. ''Come on, let's see if you can do the job of getting me pregnant.'' She led him to the creek and upstream twenty yards past where Cormac whickered in recognition.

Sometime earlier Ella had been there and had cut

down some small brush and piled up some pine boughs and covered them with two heavy comforters. She sat down on the blankets and held out her arms.

A full moon splashed light through leaves and dappled her form.

Canyon sat beside her. "You're a persistent lady," he said, his lips brushing her cheek.

"Don't know about that, but I fancy you, Canyon." She smiled and kissed him. When she came away she sighed. "Glory, I bet you got a stick down there that would choke a horse. I aim to find out." Both her hands caressed his crotch, then opened the buttons quickly and one hand worked inside.

"He's hard already," she squealed.

"I better tell you right off, Ella, he does like girls, all parts of girls."

Ella kissed him again and pulled him down on the blanket on top of her. Her large breasts cushioned his landing.

"Bet he likes all three of my holes, what would you think?"

"Best to give it a try, then decide," O'Grady said.

"You Irish? You don't talk Irish. I knew this Irish kid back on the outside. He liked to, you know, to fuck. And he had a real Irish accent."

"Well, lass, a man tends to lose the accent if he doesn't work at it." The words came out dripping with dew from the Old Country, and she laughed.

O'Grady's hand unbuttoned her blouse between them and one of her bare breasts confronted him.

"She likes you," Ella said, grinning up at him.

"She better, or I'll eat her alive."

"Good, try it."

He nuzzled down, kissed the pointed red nipple that had swelled to twice its normal size. He licked it, then around her large pink areola, then kissed the globe.

Ella moaned. "Nice, so good. Have an early breakfast right there."

Her hand closed around his erection and pulled it out of his pants. "Damn, what a fence post you've got here, lad."

"The better to satisfy you with, Ella."

She pushed him away and they sat up and stripped off their clothes. Neither said a word as they raced to get undressed. Then she sat beside him, holding his stiff penis in her hand and watching him.

"Chew on my girls some more," she said.

He bent and obliged, moving from one to the other. When he nibbled her nipple, Ella climaxed. She caught him and pulled him on top of her as she lay down. Her hips pounded upward at him and her whole body shook and rattled as one series of spasms after another ripped through her. She moaned and shrilled and gasped as the climaxes continued. He counted four in a row. At last she tapered off.

She looked up at him, her eyes wide. "Goddamn! No man ever set me off that way before he got inside me. Oh, glory, what's that going to be like?"

She pulled his hand down to her crotch and spread her legs. One of her hands found his erection again and hung on while the other hand investigated his heavy scrotum.

His fingers probed higher. Her hips lifted to his hand and he rubbed with the palm of his hand over her mound, round and round with his fingertips brushing her outer lips and bringing soft kitten sounds from her.

She moved his hand to her clit and he found the right spot and rubbed a half-dozen times. Ella squealed and drove into another climax that was stiff and sudden and ended just as quickly.

"Oh, damn," she said. Tears squeezed out of her eyes. "That one was twice as powerful as the others. You do me good, Canyon. You play me like a girl fiddle."

His fingers moved down and stroked around her outer lips, then closer, and soon he found the wetness and she purred to him as she began to pump his penis back and forth with her talented hand.

He touched her fingers holding his rod. "Easy on that, or we'll lose some," he said. She stopped and bit his ear.

His finger probed inside her wet spot gently, and when she sighed again, he rammed his finger into her vagina as far as he could.

"Yes, yes. Right now," Ella cried. She pulled him over one leg and lifted both knees, cradling him on her soft white thighs.

"Do me good, O'Grady. Fuck me like I'm the first girl you ever poked and make it last all night if you can."

He lifted back, adjusted himself, and settled down easing into the soft wetness, letting the juices gather and lubricate him, then he edged in a little at a time until she wailed and he stroked forward hard.

"Oh, Lord! Oh, Lord!" She pushed back and looked at him wide-eyed. "Lordy, no cock's ever been inside me that far. You touched something in there that gave me a real jolt. Goddamn, I won't ever forget this fucking."

"Darling Ella, we're just getting started." He worked her slowly at first, easing in and out, then drilled twenty times and stopped.

She looked up. "You done?"

"Just starting. You said to make it last." He rested, let his level of excitement ease off a little. Then he worked again pounding in a side-to-side motion that set her on fire, and Ella climaxed again, humping her hips high off the blanket as she squealed and roared until he was sure her ma could hear her in the cabin if she had the window open.

When her climax trailed off, Canyon picked up Ella's sturdy legs and lifted them high so they rested on his shoulders and she was bent nearly in half.

Now he had a different angle at her and he drove

forward easy until she felt the change and she shrilled in delight.

"I never been poked this way before. It's wild."

It also made her tighter, and before he could stop, Canyon boiled over and slammed a dozen hard strokes into her willing vagina until he had spent his seed shooting it deep inside her. He collapsed on her, let her legs down, and rested.

"Goddamn," Ella said, then closed her eyes and caught her breath as well.

They dropped off to sleep, still lanced together. But soon she woke Canyon and pointed to the moon.

"The old moon says it's a good time for breeding. You ready for another planting time? Hope so, but first, I'm hungry. You can't deny a girl a light snack."

She moved and wiped him off with her blouse, then bent over his crotch and took his quickly hardening penis in her mouth. O'Grady wasn't so jaded that such personalized treatment didn't affect him. Before he knew it, she was bobbing up and down on him as he lay on his back. His hips worked against her motion and he was amazed that she wasn't choking.

A dozen more strokes and the floodgates opened, and then there was no way he could stop the surging, driving force of the downstream flow that he jolted into her mouth in six glorious spasms.

She licked him dry, then lifted and kissed him. "Now that's what I'd call a fine snack. Of course it doesn't help a girl get pregnant. You've got to fuck me at least five more times in the old cunt to get that job done. I've heard the sixth time is the lucky one."

As it turned out, they made it through four more lovemakings, then both dropped on the blanket and neither awoke before the rooster crowed as dawn lighted the henhouse near the cabin.

Ella sat up and smiled. "Glad it wasn't cold last night." She watched him. "You all right?"

"I feel great, but I'm mad at the damn king and today we're going to start taking apart his kingdom."

"Good! Can I help? I can seduce the colonel."

"No, then he'd find some reason to give you punishment. You keep your pretty little ass right here on the farm until I come back."

She laughed and kissed him. "One quick little old fuck this morning?"

"No, you better get back to your bedroom and I'll be along shortly. I'm going to get Cormac and ride into the hills above the palace. Do you know if there are guards up there?"

"I've heard there are lots of them. But if they had guards everywhere they say they do, there would be a lot more than twenty, wouldn't there?"

"I'd say so. That's why I'm going to go take a look. You see if you can find me some breakfast. I want to get moving before most of the folks are up between here and the mountain."

Canyon guessed it was about three miles to the edge of the timber. He could stay in the brush of one creek or another most of the way.

Neither of them had dressed yet. Ella reached over and kissed his limp tool and giggled at the way he jumped and twitched. O'Grady fondled her hanging breasts, then moved and began to pull on his clothes.

"Time to move, young lady. Get dressed, or I'll be in the cabin before you are."

He had a quick breakfast of three eggs, country-fried potatoes and onions, biscuits and pan chicken gravy, and three cups of coffee. He had told Cuzick only that he was going to make a ride around the edge of the valley to see what he could learn.

"I'll stay in cover whenever I can, but it might do a little good if a stranger on a horse is reported. Get the king's men all riled up a mite so I can see where they are and where they keep their weapons."

"I've heard the guns are all in a locked room on the

first floor of the castle," Cuzick said. "The royal family lives on the second floor. I don't know what's on the two top floors."

Canyon had one more helping of biscuits and gravy and then ran for his mount in the willows along the small creek.

Cormac greeted him and took his quart of oats with relish. After drinking about ten gallons of water, the palomino was ready. Canyon rode upstream on the little creek, making it within half a mile of the timbered slopes of the mountain before he had to burst from the last concealment and head for the forest cover of tall piñon and Douglas fir.

He made it without anyone seeing him, he thought. At least he didn't see anyone and there was no cabin anywhere near him. No traffic was on the trail to the outside when he crossed it. He charged fifty yards into the woods, then stopped, tied Cormac, and ran back to the edge of the woods to study the valley.

It was larger than the had thought, perhaps fifteen miles long. He was in the lower quarter of it and could see it stretch out to misty blue ridges far to the northwest. As he watched, he could see two nearby cabins to the north come to life. Smoke issued straight up from chimneys; men and women stirred, went to the outhouses, stretched, and began to get ready for the day's work. Nowhere did he see any horses. How did they plow and plant?

O'Grady lay there a moment more, taking in the feel of the mountains. He'd been in the Rocky Mountains before, but the size, the scope, the beauty of them made him draw in a quick breath. It made him feel at home, back in the wilderness, where nature held the key until man disrupted things. He saw a swallow heading toward a new nest with twigs in its mouth.

With a small groan Canyon arose and went back to Cormac. He rode along the edge of the woods. Here and there he found spots where fir and pine had been cut to make the cabins. Farther along he found where a great number of larger trees had been felled, perhaps to build the castle.

The trees thinned and he rode deeper into the woods and up the slope for good cover. When he came down, he found the village just ahead. Again he waited at the edge of the woods, watching to see what he could learn.

He didn't see much that helped. He saw no one on horseback. He did spot a pair of draft horses in harness pulling a high-boxed farm wagon. Perhaps the horses for farmwork were kept in one barn and sent out each day for work and taken back each night.

He moved again working through the edge of the woods so he could look out at the center of the village.

Canyon soon found himself nearing the castle. There was no reason to get Cormac too near to danger such as the castle presented. There must be guards. He took the big palomino deeper into the forest and tied him, then gave him a scratch and a pat on the neck.

"Stay here awhile, Cormac, lad. I'll go see what I can find out." He hurried away, working silently through the trees. When he could at last see the top and back of the castle, Canyon stopped and lay next to a giant Douglas fir and watched. Where were the guards? There had to be some around. He lay there for half an hour and saw nothing move in the woods or at the back of the palace. He was about to get up when he saw a man leave shadows at the near side of the castle and walk into the edge of the woods and relieve himself. Then the man hurried back to his post.

So the guards were on the edge of the castle, not in the woods. That helped. He spotted a second guard near the back of the castle then and waited to see what they would do.

Before they moved again, he heard activity in the castle. He looked up at the second floor and saw a door open on a small balcony. A young woman stepped out and leaned on the log that formed the top rail around the open space. She shook out her long blond hair. Canyon guessed that this must be the same girl he had seen last night, Princess Melissa.

He wondered how in the world he could get up there to talk to her without the guards seeing him?

5

Canyon O'Grady watched the girl for several minutes. She combed out her hair, let it flutter in the wind, then stood and stared into the wood. She seemed slender, trim, and young from where he stood. She had on no royal robes or trains now, and the simple frock revealed more of her young body.

Canyon knew she might be gone at any moment. How could he get up there to ask her about her crazy father? He felt there might be some hope that she would help put an end to all of this insanity—at least if he had read her mood correctly last night.

But he could figure out no easy way to get to the balcony, especially with two armed guards scanning every inch of the rear of the palace. The wall itself would not be impossible to climb. The huge logs had been fitted together and partly flattened with axes along the sides, but there were plenty of knots and bumps and knobs where he could get footholds and handholds to work up to the second-floor balcony.

If only the damn guards weren't there . . .

The sun shone brightly now, beaming down on him through the leaves. The thought jolted at him in an instant. If he couldn't get to her, maybe she would come to him.

How could he communicate with her? The sun! Yes, he still carried a square of shiny metal with him that he had used for years as a mirror when he was in the woods and wanted to shave. He pulled out the shiny metal from a shirt pocket and polished it.

He moved to where the sun came down through a spot in the trees, and then he crawled to the very front of the woods, some thirty yards from the back of the palace.

He took the square of metal and aimed it to the side to check on the flash, and found where it was. Then he turned to the princess. She was still there. Canyon aimed the sunspot on the brush in front of him and then lifted it so it hit the wood railing, then higher so the square of bright white light touched the princess and moved across her head. She turned her face. She looked back at the woods, and the light spot brushed across her eyes. She blinked and held up her hand. At once he aimed the light high over her head, then he brought it down and flashed her in the eyes again.

Princess Melissa seemed to frown, then shielded her eyes and stared at where she had seen the flash. Slowly he stood. She could see him plainly, but he was hidden on the sides so the guards couldn't spot him. Canyon motioned for her to come, waving her toward him. At first she shook her head.

He nodded and waved for her to come again, then sank down out of sight in the ferns and tall grasses of the forest floor.

O'Grady watched through the leaves. She lifted one hand to her mouth, stared at where he had been, and then with a look of what he hoped was determination, she turned and walked back into her room.

Canyon waited, watching both sides of the castle. He could see no doors in the back of the big structure. How long could he wait? Could a contingent of the Royal Guards be slipping up on him from both sides right this instant?

He climbed a young Engelmann spruce and broke a bough to hold in front of himself and put one below him so it would be virtually impossible to see him from the ground. Canyon sat there less than fifteen feet off the ground, but in a fine position to watch the castle and the two guards.

Now, with daylight, the sentries began walking posts. They walked toward the middle of the castle until they met, where they saluted each other and returned to the far side of the castle where they had begun. This maneuver was repeated continuously.

After what seemed like an hour but probably was less than ten minutes, Canyon saw a woman come around the corner of the castle. She timed it just right so the two guards were facing each other and not looking behind. They saluted and by the time they talked a moment and turned around, the woman was safely in the cover of the woods. It was Princess Melissa.

O'Grady waited. He could hear her coming through the trees and the light underbrush. This princess was not a woodsman. He dropped from his perch to the ground and went to meet her to cut down the distance she had to go and the noise she made.

He rounded a big Douglas fir tree and saw her ten feet ahead. She had just caught her shawl on a branch and it had pulled the garment partway off her shoulders.

O'Grady cleared his throat softly.

She heard and looked up. "You? Who are you and how are you so bold as to beckon to me?"

"May I come to help you?"

She frowned a moment, then nodded. He moved through the ten feet without making a sound, and she looked up, surprised.

"How can you walk in the woods so silently?"

"Practice, Princess Melissa." He stopped beside her, unsnarled the shawl from the tangle of the underbrush, and redraped it over her shoulders. "You asked me who I am. I am a newcomer to your valley, and I don't like what's happening here. I saw the punishment last night."

Her face clouded. "How dare you criticize the king. How could you . . ." Her voice trailed off.

"I could tell that you were horrified by what the King did. The punishment is cruel. Your father is not well. He needs to be helped, not to be ruling all these people."

Suddenly long-suppressed tears rolled down her cheeks as she cried silently. He held out his arms and she fell against him, weeping and sobbing, clinging to him.

"Melissa, I have come to help the people, to free them."

She looked up through her tears. Her eyes were soft blue, her skin a fragile light pink that made him think of peaches and cream. Little by little, she stopped crying, but she still held to him. Her face with its small tipped-up nose nestled against his chest. She was as cute as a two-day-old colt.

"But what can one man do?" she asked, looking up at him. "Even to talk of rebellion is a death sentence."

"There are ways. Will you help me?"

"What can I do? He's my father."

"But he's ill, he's out of his mind. You know it's true. He almost died in the army in Texas when his company was overrun. That day he went half-crazy, you know this, Melissa."

"You—you know about the Comanches?"

"Yes. I'm here to help him, if he'll let me. If not, I'll help the people he's imprisoned."

"The guards will catch you and kill you. Just talking to me is a capital offense. I—"

"They won't catch me. I can defend myself." He lifted the army percussion revolver he had retrieved from its hiding spot before he rode from the creek that morning and showed it to her.

"Oh, dear! That too, is a capital offense."

"I know. Where are the king's weapons stored?"

"In a room just inside the front doors of the palace on the first floor. There are three locks on the doors."

"How many fighting men does Colonel Daniel have? Only the twenty in the Royal Guards?"

"No, more. With all of the supervisors it would be almost forty."

"Do they all have rifles?"

"No. I've heard Daddy and the colonel talking about that. They have only the twenty rifles—no, twenty-one now counting the one they brought on the last stagecoach." Her eyes brightened. "Oh, now I see how you got in. You followed the wagon in from the Denver road."

"You're not only a beautiful princess, you're quick and smart as well. Yes, it seemed a good way to find out where this King of Colorado had his kingdom."

She smiled. "Oh, I didn't tell you. Touching the princess is another capital offense." As she said it, she snuggled closer and put her arms around him, holding him tight.

"I must be dead a dozen times by now, then, pretty colleen."

She looked at him and moved her head to see him better. That placed their faces close together. She clung to him. "What's your name?"

"Canyon O'Grady. I'm working for the President of the United States. The raiders have been stealing stagecoaches that carry U.S. mail. That's what got the federal people all excited, and is what brought me here."

"Canyon O'Grady. What an interesting name. I'll remember it always." Her mood changed. She stared hard at him, her face now serious. "Canyon O'Grady, my father is not all bad. The first three years here in the valley we struggled together and everyone accomplished a great deal. My father did a lot of good here. He had the commune running beautifully. We were self-sufficient in ninety-nine percent of our needs. The people were free and happy. We had no crime, little unhappiness, a good Christian-based community that was doing remarkably well. That was until two years ago. I hope you don't treat my father harshly. But I know this king nonsense has got to stop.''

One of the guards below called to the other one. Canyon listened carefully, but he couldn't understand the words. He could see the guards moving toward the woods.

Melissa saw them, too. "I must go. I often sneak away from the guards and walk in the woods. They scold me, but I threaten to report them and my father never hears about it. The next time you want to see me in the morning, flash your mirror, but just once. When I see it, I'll comb my hair and leave.''

She held him tightly. "Now I have some hope. Please be careful. Don't let them catch you.'' She lifted to her tiptoes and kissed his cheek, then bent and picked some ferns and some wildflowers and rushed back toward the edge of the woods.

Princess Melissa sang a little song and picked more flowers at the edge of the woods in plain sight of the two guards. They walked over and talked to her softly, gently, and she smiled at them, gave each a flower, and then walked back to the side of the palace and vanished around it.

When the bored guards were back at their posts and walking their paths, O'Grady slid deeper into the woods to where he had left Cormac. He patted the big stallion and let the palomino rub his eyes gently against the softness of Canyon's shirt. It was a way the horse could clear out irritants from his eyes. There was no natural softness for him to use. When the big horse was satisfied, he lifted his head and snorted softly.

O'Grady mounted, and he and Cormac worked around the edge of the woods for half a mile observing the village. He saw a well-equipped blacksmith shop, a tinsmith, a furniture shop, and a market where fruits and vegetables were either sold or parceled out. Farther along he found the livery stable, where, evidently, all of the horses in the kingdom, except those of the cowboys, were kept at night.

Now and then a farmer would arrive and leave with a team pulling a wagon or some other farm machinery.

O'Grady was nearly at the end of the village when he saw a well-traveled wagon road that lead into the hills up a small canyon. As he watched from deep in the woods, a wagon went up the road with a dozen picks and shovels in the back and two buckets that must hold thirty to forty gallons. They seemed to be made of heavy metal.

Canyon followed the wagon, staying out of sight in the brush along the side of the road. The wagon soon met another coming down the track and each moved over on the narrow road. When they were even, they stopped and the drivers talked.

The U.S. agent couldn't quite hear what they were saying. A moment later they waved and continued on their journey.

Over half an hour later they came to the end of the road and Canyon had a hard time finding cover for Cormac. At last he tied him in some heavy brush and worked forward on foot. When he saw where he was, he nodded.

Three men with rifles stood guard over six men who panned for gold and worked sluice boxes in the cold water of the creek. Another hundred feet above, four men worked with picks and shovels starting a tunnel into the face of the cliff. Canyon looked up and saw an upthrust of rock.

Evidently someone thought this was the source of the mother lode that had produced free gold in the stream below.

Gold was one easy way to pay wages to keep the

guards and supervisors in line. But a little free gold from six pans wouldn't be enough to subjugate three hundred people for long.

O'Grady worked back through the brush to his horse, mounted, and rode back toward the main valley. The gold strike would be another asset for this new community if it ever could become free. He hid Cormac in the brush again and tied his gun belt and 1860 army revolver to the saddle, then walked down a short lane into the village.

He felt naked without his weapon, but he needed to know more about the inner workings of the town. He came past the livery stable and saw that they had good horses that were well-cared-for. They had hay and grain and probably oats, he decided.

Cuzick had told Canyon there were no kind of identity papers or strict daily regimen for the people in the valley. New people came in from time to time, so not even the supervisors could know everyone in their areas.

With his localized clothes, O'Grady felt he could walk around the village without being bothered. He wouldn't look out of place; he would blend in. Canyon confirmed his brief view of last night that the place was well-laid-out, that there were all the necessary goods and services for the people, and that on the surface everyone seemed to be busy and relatively happy. Except that they were all prisoners.

He was going to do something about that.

O'Grady came to a gunsmith shop and slowed. Why would they have a gunsmith in a town where none of the people could own guns? It must be from the old days. He went up to the door and started to turn the knob when a voice from behind stopped him.

"What the hell do you think you're doing?"

Canyon O'Grady turned around slowly. The voice

belonged to Waldron, the supervisor from the Cuzick farm.

"Cat got your tongue, man? I asked you what the hell you're doing trying to go into that gunsmith's shop?"

6

"What am I doing?" Canyon O'Grady asked as he stared at the red-hatted supervisor. "Nothing. Just looking. You see, I'm kind of new here and I've been out on the farm most of the last four, five weeks, and they just sent me to town to bring back the horses and now I'm a little lost. Which way is north out of town?"

"Lost? Lost? You're an addled idiot. Right behind you. Follow that street over there and it ends up in the north road. You're a dumb shithead, you know that? What's your name?"

"Nate Lerner, sir."

"Work station?"

"Farm Twenty-four, I think. Or is it Twenty-three? Never had to remember it before . . . sir."

"Okay, okay, forget it. That gun shop is stripped of everything useful and it's kept locked. Don't bother it again. Now get on out of here. You said north, so walk north."

Canyon bobbed his head in thanks and began an ambling, loose-jointed walk as he moved up the street to the north. He was a block away when he looked around. The red cap stood watching him. O'Grady pointed ahead of him and the supervisor nodded. He kept walking.

He went up another block, and when he glanced back, the supervisor was gone. Canyon saw nothing else that interested him. The rest of the shops were artisans and merchants, but evidently all goods and food were without charge. They still functioned on a commune basis in the kingdom. It had worked well before, why not continue it and only change the government?

The U.S. agent slipped around a bakery and ran down the next block, then worked toward the edge of town to the left and the woods. He had seen enough of the "downtown" section of the kingdom. He still had to work out some kind of an attack plan that would disable most of the twenty gunners, or their guns, and give the citizens a chance to rise up and smash down the supervisors. Mere numbers alone could do the job—if the Royal Guards with their Henry repeating rifles could be dealt with.

O'Grady was about a block from the castle when he saw a figure ahead standing beside what had once been a small shoe factory. Now the place was closed. It was a woman in dark clothes and a big sunbonnet that covered most of her face.

She seemed no threat, so he walked toward the woman. He had almost passed when he looked closer. She stared at him, then crooked her finger at him. She turned and walked into the small door of the shoe factory, looking back once to see if he followed.

As she turned he saw her smile.

Princess Melissa.

He hurried into the semidarkness of the shuttered building. She had stopped just inside the door and now watched him a minute.

"Canyon O'Grady, you are a hard man to find. I had one of the guards, Robert, looking all over for you. He saw you just as one of the supervisors caught you at the gun shop. That's one of the forbidden places in the village."

The princess closed the door, pushing a sliding bolt firmly into the framing that locked the door. She moved to one of the windows and opened a blind a little to let in enough light so they could see.

"Canyon, I had to see you before tomorrow morning. Robert is a guard at the castle who works for me. I pay him and he tells me anything I want to know."

"Does this Robert have access to information?"

"The guards are told what is planned so that they can help. Today he said there is to be an expedition. Colonel Daniel will take twenty men, half Royal Guards and half citizens with military training, and form them into an assault force.

"Within three days the men will leave on an attempt to capture the small town of Fort Collins, and to use it as the king's base for his northern provinces."

"But you said he only had twenty guns. There must be a hundred men in Fort Collins by now, and they all have two or three guns each. The attackers would be wiped out."

"They have a plan. They will steal guns from as many of the people as they can, then store them and do battle."

"That would be a better plan, but it still can't work."

"My father and Colonel Daniel have planned it well. Remember, both of them are well-trained military men."

"How will they get the citizens to fight? Won't they run away or turn on their officers?"

"No. The men's wives and children living here will be held hostage in the meeting hall until the fighters return."

"That would be one way." Canyon scowled. "Dammit! So fast. That pushes up my timetable by a lot."

"You must do something to stop them. Colonel Daniel will go with the troops, but my father will stay here. I'm afraid that many people will die. The king is still angry at some of the people in Fort Collins who treated us badly while we lived there. He will not be nice to them if he captures the town."

57

She moved toward him, stood close, and looked at him.

O'Grady put his arms around her, pulled her firm body tightly against his, and kissed her waiting lips. Her arms circled him and held him fast. The kiss ended and she reached up and kissed him again.

"Darling Canyon, you must do something before a lot of people die."

"I will, but you're a pleasing distraction. I need to meet with this Robert friend of yours. Can you arrange it?"

"Of course. Robert will do anything I ask him to."

"Good. Tonight in back of the castle. I'll be there just as it gets dark."

"He'll be there." Melissa looked up at Canyon. "It's so good to be alone. I disguise myself sometimes and Robert helps me and we walk around the village. But this is better. You and I are alone. I—I would like you to kiss me again."

O'Grady took care of the request, his tongue brushing her lips and bringing a small gasp of surprise from her. She made pleased noises in her throat, then moved back from him. She caught his hand and put it over her breast.

"Would you touch me there as we kiss? I've dreamed of someone doing that for so long. You'll never know. Father won't let a man come anywhere near me. I've never even been kissed before today."

Canyon kissed her again, and this time, when his tongue brushed her lips, they came open. His hand rubbed her soft breast gently, then his fingers worked a button loose on her blouse and crept inside. A moment later his hand closed around her bare breast and she gasped, then shuddered and almost climaxed. Her breath came in hot, short pants as he rubbed her warm breast.

"Oh, my," she said softly as the kiss ended. "Leave your hand there, please. It's so wonderful. I feel so warm and good and—and almost like I'm melting. Right now I want to lie down and let you—let you do anything you want to.'' She pushed him away. ''But I can't. Robert is outside waiting. He was to rap on the door if there was any danger and we've been here too long now. Thank you, my darling, for the kiss and the caress. Robert will meet you tonight just at dark. Keep safe.'' She kissed him quickly, caught his hand, and hurried to the door.

She went out first, making sure no one saw her. Canyon saw a man waiting a short distance away. He was not in a guard uniform. After they walked away, O'Grady stepped out of the door, threw the outside bolt, and walked off in the other direction.

What would he do until dark? He remembered about the mess hall that still served those who did not cook at home. It was mostly for men who had no families. The place was near the other end of town. He went by the side streets and found it. Already it was nearly five in the afternoon.

It reminded him of the mess hall on a big ranch he once worked on. It was a large building, with the kitchen on one end, a food line he went through with a tray, and then long wooden benches and tables where he sat down and ate. The food was good. Fried chicken, mashed potatoes and gravy, green beans, thick slabs of bread, and coffee. He pushed his empty tray and silverware into a tub of hot water and wandered outside.

Down the street he saw two red-hatted supervisors coming, and he faded into an alley and hurried toward the woods where he could hide until dark.

Canyon found Cormac where he had left him, strapped on his six-gun, and felt more at ease. Three days. He still hadn't seen the key element he needed, the one weak spot where he could strike and turn this monarchy into a small battleground and a big victory for democracy. But he'd find it.

He gave Cormac a drink, then some oats from one of the saddlebags, and tied the stallion. O'Grady lay down for a short nap. It was nearly dark when he awoke. He had come within two hundred yards of the back of the castle. Now he left Cormac with a slap on the neck and worked silently through the high-mountain timber toward the castle.

He was there just as the last of the darkness slid over the gentle valley. O'Grady went up into his favorite Engelmann spruce and climbed fifteen feet off the ground. When the guard came, he stopped below Canyon.

The agent dropped out of the limbs and had his six-inch sheath knife at the guard's throat before the man could turn around. "Don't scream. What's your name?"

"Robert. The princess said you wanted to see me."

"That I do, lad. We have some talking and then some work to do. Would a small libation ease the way a little between us?" O'Grady withdrew the knife carefully and the man nodded.

Canyon took out a thin flask of Irish whiskey and offered it to the man. Robert grinned.

"The princess said you were an Irishman. Never met an Irishman I didn't like. But then you're my first," Robert grinned, then sipped at the Irish whiskey.

"Mighty fine, but you don't have to bribe me. I'm dead set on helping the princess to get out of this mess without being killed. You say you can be of some aid?"

"We can help each other. I'm here to turn this kingdom into another county in the Territory of Colorado."

"Freedom, that sounds good. I'm interested as long as your plan sets these people free."

"Indeed it will, Robert. Now, first I'll need to get

to those twenty Henry rifles. I want to break off the firing pins in all twenty. How can we do that?''

Robert grinned. "I'm beginning to like the way your mind works. Why have a shoot-out with twenty Henry repeating rifles if you don't have to? Yes, I can easily get you into the weapons room late some night.''

"Good, good. Then we'll need to find all of the spare firing pins for the weapons. Next I'll need to locate the powder magazine and hope there's at least two kegs of black powder there.''

"Fact is, there's six kegs. Back before the king, we used to use the powder to blow stumps out of the ground to plant more crops. Haven't done that lately.''

"Can you get me to the rifles and to the powder? I'll want the powder first for preparations. Then the rifles will be, how shall we say it, adjusted, the night before we launch our big takeover.''

"Won't be easy, but I can do it. Have to crack one guard's skull, but I've never liked the guy anyway. There'll be some stink about it the next morning, though.''

"Just so we can get it. We might as well start tonight. Are you on duty now?''

"Nope, tonight's my night off.''

"Good, there must be a room full of the pistols and rifles and shotguns the people in the commune had. Did the king confiscate them?''

"Oh, yeah. Over two years ago when he got real tough. It was a hanging offense to have a weapon. I'll have to find out where they were put.''

"First the powder. Where is it? In the castle?''

"Right you are. Wish we had at least a six-gun.''

Canyon held up his 1860 army percussion revolver, and the guard yelped in surprise. "I've altered this revolver so the cylinder snaps in and out. I can fire five or six shots, snap out the fired cylinder, and push in one with six fresh rounds and go right on firing. Surprises a lot of good gunmen who think I'm out of rounds. I always carry two cylinders with five rounds loaded and ready to go.''

''I'll be damned.'' Robert shook his head. ''Never heard of such a thing. Now, when we get them two kegs of black powder, where the hell do we hide them? Things weigh about forty pounds each.''

''I'll pick out a command center for them. What time will be best to go in there?''

''About three in the morning. The midnight guard is getting tired by then and we'll take him easy. I'll get my uniform on so he'll think I'm replacing him or something.''

''But don't let him see your face.''

''Right, otherwise I'm on the run with you.''

O'Grady kicked the ground and moved a pair of stones, then lay down. ''Time to get some sleep so we don't get caught taking that powder.''

''Damn, if I lie down, I'm liable to sleep until dawn,'' Robert said.

''Not a chance, my boot will be in your ribs rousting you out.''

By three-fifteen that morning they were at the front door of the palace. There was no outside guard this late. The inside man was supposed to be standing directly behind the locked front door.

Robert knocked on the door. It cracked open an inch. O'Grady slammed into the unlatched door with his shoulder and blasted the inside guard back four feet; he slammed him to the floor and knocked him out. Canyon was on him in a second, his forearm pressing across his throat. The guard was gagged, blindfolded, bound, and put to one side.

''Down this way,'' Robert whispered. They hurried along the plank floors of the castle, down half-round log stairs to a small cellar where a pair of sturdy padlocks secured the heavy log door.

Robert had grabbed the key ring from the guard and

now opened the door. Inside, they felt their way along the walls.

"Wish I could strike a match, but the whole place might blow up," Robert said. He found the powder, handed a keg to Canyon, and picked up one himself. They locked the door and hurried back to the big lobby. Robert took his keg out the front door at once.

O'Grady stopped and untied the guard and took off the blindfold and gag. The man was still unconscious. Canyon hurried toward the front door and almost bumped into a Royal Guard in his red hat and jacket.

The guard held a revolver in his right hand and had a big grin on his face. "Well, well, I had a feeling something was going to go wrong tonight," the lieutenant said. "Damn good thing I came down here to check."

Canyon looked at the revolver. The hammer was in full cock and the lieutenant's finger caressed the trigger with practiced ease.

"Just put down the powder and turn around and put your hands behind you. Then we'll find out who you are and what the hell you were going to do with forty pounds of black powder."

7

"What I'm doing with the black powder?" Canyon O'Grady asked the man in front of him with the cocked revolver. "Hell, sir, the captain told me to come get it, guess you'll have to ask him what he's gonna do with it."

"Good try, but we don't have a captain of the guard," the lieutenant snarled. "I'm the commanding officer. Put down the powder gently. Now!" The six-gun came up and leveled at O'Grady's heart.

Behind the lieutenant, the outside door opened silently and Robert came in with a stick of firewood.

"Yes, sir, like to put it down, but dammit, it's my shoulder. Been having trouble with it. We wouldn't want to drop the damn keg and have it blow up, now would we?" Robert had slipped up under the sound of O'Grady's voice and slammed the three-inch-thick split of wood down on the lieutenant's head. The officer's eyes fell shut and he crumpled to the floor.

"Thanks," Canyon whispered. Already Robert had bent down and grabbed the revolver from the officer's hand and run for the door. They both slipped outside where Robert picked up his keg. Canyon carried his own keg of black powder and followed the smaller man toward the woods.

They ran again as best they could with the heavy kegs of powder. Once in the cover of the brush and trees, they stopped and rested.

"Where are we taking this stuff?" Robert asked.

"I don't have the faintest idea. Somewhere so I can find it again when I want it."

"You're going to blow up the castle?"

"No. I don't want to ruin anything unless I can't help it. Maybe a small demonstration explosion would be good."

"Why?"

"To start the official revolt of the masses. Which has to be within three days, from what you told Melissa."

"That's what the colonel said to us this morning. The attack on Fort Collins will leave here in three days."

"Where do the Royal Guards sleep?"

"First floor, down those two long halls you saw."

"Could we lock them in the barracks, rooms, whatever?"

"Not a chance. All have windows they could break out."

"Where do the supervisors and you guards live?"

"Third floor. We use the back stairway. It doesn't open onto the second floor."

"And nobody has guns but the Royal Guards?"

"Right, and about half the time they don't have any rounds in those Henry repeaters."

"Well, now, that's a good bit of information. But we can't depend on that. If it comes to a fight they will have rounds. Do the men clean those weapons, take them apart and oil them, that sort of thing?"

"Almost never. They don't fire them enough to need it."

"Good, then they won't find the broken firing pins." O'Grady looked into the woods. "Now, let's find a good place to hide this powder until we need it."

They put the powder behind a four-foot-thick Douglas fir and scraped a small hole and covered it with brush and leaves.

"Now, Robert, you better get back to your barracks.

65

I'll be pleased to have your help anytime you want to participate.''

The smaller man nodded, waved, and ran back toward the castle.

O'Grady walked back to where he had left Cormac and stroked the golden horse's neck. What else could he do tonight to slow down the expected attack on Fort Collins?

He would certainly want to drive every horse in the livery barn as far into the north end of the valley as he could before they were to leave on the attack. But tonight was too early.

Disabling the rifles was the key. Then a rebellion of the people would be possible. The people . . . How would they know about it? He could play like he was Paul Revere and ride through the streets shouting the news. Possible. He was getting groggy. It was far too late to go back to the Cuzicks'. Better he make a bed here and get some rest.

Canyon stepped into the saddle and rode Cormac another two hundred yards into the woods, found a level spot, and settled down for the rest of the night.

Hell-to-pay time came before morning back at the castle. Lieutenant Zellmer slowly regained consciousness. He realized he lay facedown on the floor. Why? Then he remembered the tall man with the keg of powder.

They had been robbed! He stabbed for his revolver, but it wasn't in its holster. Then he remembered: he had had it out covering the robber, but now it was gone. He was in trouble.

Slowly he pushed away from the floor and sat up. His head pounded like a million church bells all at once. The castle entryway wobbled and whirled and at last came to a stop. Now the pain daggered into his brain and he reached down to steady himself.

Somebody stole a keg of black powder, and his revolver. Who? Malcontents? What about the guard who should be on duty? Zellmer looked around and at last found a pair of feet extending from behind a chair. Zellmer crawled over to the spot and found the guard coming back to consciousness.

The lieutenant had to get help. It took him three tries, but at last he held on to the table and stood. Three wobbly steps later and he was feeling better. He walked with only a little vertigo to the guard head-quarters halfway down the hall and rousted out two more men to cover the front door, inside and out.

When Zellmer went back to check on the guard who had been knocked out, the man sat against the wall holding his head.

"It all happened so fast," the recovering guard said. "The door smashed in and knocked me down and I passed out. When I came to I was tied up. Then I passed out again."

"Did you see anyone?"

"Just a flash of somebody outside."

Zellmer asked the man for his key ring. It was gone. The head of the Royal Guards felt the foundation dropping out from under his position. How could he tell the king that he had let at least two men break into the castle, knock out him and a guard, steal a keg of black powder, a six-gun revolver, and the key ring to the whole castle? He couldn't. The king would never know.

"Guard, not a word about this to anyone. It won't go on your record. You'll forget anything happened. If someone asks, you had a fainting spell from some bad food. Now, I'll help you to your quarters."

Lieutenant Zellmer thought about the man he had seen. Over six feet tall, well over, maybe six-four. Flame-red hair that couldn't be missed, and the man probably weighing 220 pounds. A hard man to miss in a crowd.

The lieutenant took his own keys and hurried down

to the powder magazine in the basement. He unlocked the door and counted the kegs by touch. He found there were only four left. Two had been stolen. Now, if he could just keep it all quiet . . . The king must not know. And Colonel Daniel must never know.

The lieutenant went back upstairs, pulled in the outside guard, and sent him back to the guard room. Everything would be just as it was. A man got ill and was replaced. Nothing unusual about that. He'd have one more talk with that guard, Balsam was his name. And that should take care of it.

By the time Lieutenant Zellmer had his story straight, it was after four o'clock in the morning. He went back to bed for three hours and reported to Colonel Daniel's quarters promptly at eight, ready for any assignments. The colonel nibbled on his breakfast while sitting up in his bed.

"Zellmer, how was the night, quiet?"

"Yes, sir—as usual. We have the peasants well in hand."

"That's not exactly the way I hear it, Zellmer." Colonel Daniel scowled at his subordinate. His dark eyes glowed, his brow furrowed, his lips pinched into a thin dangerous line that turned down on the ends. "You want to tell me what happened last night, or shall I tell you?"

"One of my men became ill and had to be replaced. He passed out from bad food, we think. That was just after three A.M."

"Bend down here, Zellmer," the colonel said. Zellmer did, wondering what would happen. The colonel reached up and ripped his shoulder boards off his uniform one after the other. "You're demoted to private, Zellmer. If you're going to bribe your people, make it worth their while. Lieutenant Balsam is your replacement. I know Balsam was surprised and injured last night by one or two intruders. I know that he was bound and gagged and that you evidently were also on the scene and revived him. What I want to know is what happened in between.''

Zellmer stood ramrod-stiff. He had done two years in the U.S. Army before he deserted. He knew the enlisted man's code of silence. Now he was a private again.

"What happened, Zellmer?''

"Nothing, sir. I found him unconscious; I replaced him and sent him to his quarters. Balsam is lying to get a promotion.''

"And you're not? Get out of here, Zellmer. I'm changing your status. You're no longer in the Royal Guards. You've been reassigned to the stables, where your duty is to clean the shit out of the horse stalls for the next ten years. Now get out!''

Zellmer turned and silently left.

Colonel Daniel sat in his bed finishing his breakfast and thinking about Zellmer. He'd handled it a bit too harshly. He should have found out what was stolen or who escaped from the palace or what went on just after the guard was knocked out. Now Zellmer would gladly die rather than tell him.

No great loss. He'd find out some other way. He had sent one of his runners to check on the gun and ammunitions room. Had the robbers tried to get into the guns?

The man came back with a response from the sergeant who slept inside the gun room. No one had bothered him, the guns and weapons and ammunition were all accounted for. Everything was secure.

What else would a robber try to steal? The rifles were the key elements, and the civilian guns they had confiscated two years ago. No, it must be something else. The king's quarters had not been approached. The guards there had confirmed that.

Colonel Daniel would watch and wait and listen. Nothing must interfere with the attack on Fort Collins.

Once that small town was captured, he would become General Daniel and he would be governor of the northern provinces. The small community of Loveland would be swallowed up on the way and they would own a long stretch of the Denver road. Anyone passing in either direction would pay a toll and the governor would have exclusive rights to all that revenue.

Yes, nothing must interfere with the assault on Fort Collins. Which meant the king would not be told about the break-in this morning. Nothing must stop the attack.

Colonel Daniel had been with the king for a long time. He had even been in his regiment for a time before he became dissatisfied with military life and deserted. To join him again in Fort Collins and rise to his second in command was a fine accomplishment.

Of course it would also be nice to be king.

The king was a sick man. In his more lucid moments he admitted it and said that if he were suddenly taken away by sickness, Colonel Daniel was the heir apparent and would be at once elevated to the crown.

Sickness or a .44 bullet would do the same thing. It was something to ponder on.

A young girl came in. "Are you finished with breakfast, Colonel?" she asked.

She was delightful, about fifteen and well-developed. He nodded and she came toward him. He kicked out of bed and sat on the edge of it, naked.

The girl looked at him, then down at his crotch; she blushed and glanced away.

When she bent over to pick up his tray, the colonel's hand caressed her round bottom and pressed downward between her legs. She stood still without moving. He could look down her loose blouse and saw that she wore nothing under the outer garment. Her breasts swung free, large, pink-tipped, and both in plain sight.

His right hand reached down and petted her breasts, then withdrew and he patted her bottom.

"Will there be anything else, Colonel?" she asked, her voice husky with desire.

"Not now, sweetheart. You come back this afternoon and we'll have a nap."

"Yes, sir." She picked up the breakfast tray and carried it to the door. There she turned, smiled at him sweetly, and went out the door.

Colonel Daniel laughed softly. Position produced certain privileges. The king really had a free hand. He could take his pick of the maidens of the whole village. It was his royal right and no one could raise a hand. The king certainly did more than his share of picking pretty maidens.

Colonel Daniel dressed and considered his work for the day. He had to select the twenty-three best horses they had. These would be restricted from doing any farm work until the attack on Fort Collins.

Next he would select ten civilians and train them carefully in the use of the Henry repeating rifle. He would chose them carefully, young men with pretty wives who had a whole life ahead of them and who would be eager to do anything needed so they could come back to their families.

Yes, a man learned a lot about how to handle other men in the army. Fear was man's basic motivating factor. Keep men afraid of you, and afraid for their families, even afraid for their very lives, and you could make them do anything you told them to do.

Colonel Shooter Daniel slapped a riding crop against his leg and marched out of the palace to inspect the stables and select the best horses for his troops.

8

The King of Colorado slept in that morning. He roused about eight o'clock, turned over, and went back to sleep. He had to have all of his strength for the Games, which would take place promptly at noon. Every Friday he took part in the Games, and that tired him out for a week, but it was worth it.

The Games were one of the best fringe benefits of being the King of Colorado. Oh, not of all Colorado, yet, but he was working on it. He'd soon have Fort Collins, then he'd expand all the way over to the borders of Kansas and Nebraska to the east. That way he'd pick up Greeley, a nice-size little town.

He was counting on the gold mine to strike it rich soon, and the gold would finance the thrusts into these new areas. Once captured, the areas themselves would produce revenue for him through the work of the generals he assigned each province.

It might take him ten years to get to Denver, but one of these days, Denver, too, would be his. He wasn't worried about all the talk about Colorado becoming a territory by February of next year, 1861. Hell, a territory had less law enforcement than an unorganized area like they were in now.

Klingman turned over on the silk sheets and soon drifted into another nap and a dream of the Games beginning.

* * *

The King of Colorado woke up and looked at the big windup clock beside the bed. Nearly ten o'clock. He got up. The moment his feet touched the floor, his dresser hurried in with his royal robes for the day. She was stout, about thirty, and the first day she served him she had told him not to be concerned being naked in front of her. She said she had seen more men's private parts than she cared to talk about and that they held no interest for her whatsoever.

Once he had tried to get her sexually excited, but she had ignored him and his erection until he dismissed her. After that they got along fine.

Now she selected an outfit of soft gray pants, a rich purple tunic, and a robe in a slightly darker shade of purple. He put them on at once and went to his breakfast.

During his small feast—no matter what time of the day he arose he had food waiting for him—he called in Colonel Daniel to find out how progress went for preparations for the attack on Fort Collins.

"Progressing fine, your highness. I'm selecting the best of our riding horses now for our cavalry. I expect that we will get there in two days, spend two more days and nights in reducing the number of firearms in the town as much as possible, then attack and overwhelm any defenders left the following day. A five-day campaign against the town at the very most."

"Good, good." The king finished his breakfast of pancakes and sugar syrup, three eggs, and bacon and looked up at the colonel. "Oh, this is Friday and we're having the Games today. I always ask one special person to play with me. Would you like to participate?"

The colonel brightened, then frowned. "It would be my most fervent desire to play in the Games, your highness, but I have to select my ten new cavalrymen and start training them. I have only three days left."

"Yes, yes of course." The king dismissed the colonel with a flick of his hand and a girl came and carried away the breakfast tray from the table. He stared out a large plate-glass window for a few seconds, then stood.

His dresser woman stood by the outer door waiting. King Jacob turned to her. "Let the Games begin," he bellowed. "You have five minutes to prepare the contestants."

"All is ready, your Highness. You may begin at your pleasure."

"Good, good." Klingman left the room and burst through swinging doors into a long room that had six handsome chairs arranged in a semi circle. A throne fronted them. In each of the chairs sat a nude girl between thirteen and nineteen. Some were bold, sitting tall, throwing out their chests. Others were shy, embarrassed. One was indifferent.

The king walked around the semicircle, looking carefully at each naked girl. Then he sat down on his throne. On a whispered command by his dresser, the girls stood and walked slowly past the King.

He nodded and pointed at the second one in line, a curvaceous redhead. She stepped out of line. The third girl went by and he chose the fourth, the indifferent one with the best figure of the six, a tall blonde.

The last girl in the line was now in front of him and he stopped the final two girls and looked at each, then pointed at the smallest of the six, a dark little brunette with modest breasts and slender hips.

His dresser came past the king and lifted her brows. "The king is going to be a busy man today with three."

King Jacob laughed and waved his hand and the three girls were led into his playroom. It had one massive bed in the center that was ten feet square, with a huge headboard that held all sorts of food and drink.

Klingman sat on the edge of the bed, waved the dresser out the door, and smiled at his three ladies.

"Now is the time of your lives that you'll always remember. Think of it as your first royal fuck." He laughed, and one of the girls winced. "Oh, come now, you've heard talk like that before." He snapped his fingers. "Undress me, let the Games begin."

He laughed again, and this time the redhead laughed with him and unbuckled his belt and pulled down his trousers. The others had taken off his shirt and soon he sat on the big bed as naked as they were.

The king fondled the blonde's big breasts with one hand, pulled the brunette's face down to his crotch and his growing erection with the other hand and then caressed the redhead's crotch.

"Glory, I'm going to have to work hard to have something for each of you to do."

The redhead lifted her breast to his mouth and pushed it in, then eased him down on his back as he sucked delightedly. The brunette was busy rousting his manhood to full flower. When it rose completely, she eased over him where he lay on his back and lanced him into her dark hair-protected sheath. He groaned in favor of the move. The redhead moved up beside him and he pushed his first two fingers deliciously into her vagina and she squealed half in pleasure and half in show.

For a short time the king chewed and humped upward as the brunette rode him like a wild stallion, and he spit out a tit and screeched as he fired his first shot into the brunette, pumping her pink little bottom three feet in the air and nearly toppling her off the perch.

The king panted for a minute or two, then he sat up. He grabbed the redhead and pushed her flat on her back, then he took the blonde and arranged her on top of the other girl with her face on the other's crotch.

"Make love to each other," he ordered. At first the girls frowned. Then the redhead reached up and licked a drop of juice from the blonde's nether lips which were spread wide in invitation. The blonde pulled apart the other girl's legs and spread them under her face and licked at the love lips just below.

A minute later the two were deeply involved, licking and chewing on the other, emitting little shrieks of joy. They rolled over and continued.

The brunette toyed with the king's shaft, but it was defeated for several more minutes. She shrugged and pushed him back down and sat on his chest, then inched forward until her red nether lips still oozing the king's own juices were an inch from the royal mouth. She leaned forward until she made contact.

"What the hell," the king growled and began licking juices from the rich nether lips. He found her clit and twanged it a dozen times until the girl over him shrieked in joy and spasmed in a dozen climaxes as she pressed the royal face deep into her writhing pussy lips.

Beside them the other two girls were quickly reaching the height of their desire. The redhead climaxed first as the blonde's talented tongue drilled her clit six times and set off her powder keg. When the redhead at last finished wailing and moaning, she shook her head in delight, then dived back into the delicious vagina spread before her and attacked the blonde's clit until she wailed in total release and spasmed and humped and screeched for nearly two minutes before she fell exhausted.

It was about five minutes before anyone moved. Then the king pulled all three of the naked girls over him and they tried to figure out what to do next.

"A chain, let's make a chain," the redhead shouted. "You know, each one of us doing another one and getting done in return."

They started with the king. He punched his wand into the blonde from behind. She leaned forward and pushed her face into the brunette's muff at her crotch. The redhead spread her legs wide over the brunette's face, angling back toward the king, who reached over and chewed on her breasts. The redhead stretched over and pumped two fingers up the king's rectum.

"Oh, damn, a four-way chain," King Jacob said. He worked hard to make his climax this time, and when he eased down, the women were exploding all around him. When the shrieks and sighs and moans were all over, they lay that way for another ten minutes recuperating.

Klingman sat up and looked at them. "This is the best the Games have ever been. I want all three of you back next week and we'll add three more. We can have a six-way game."

The blonde pouted. "Damn, you should have thought of that before the other three got away this time."

They all laughed and tried to figure out what to do next. Before anything happened, the king crawled to the headboard and began to eat the cheeses and fruits and cakes there.

He didn't want to admit it, but twice was his limit, and he had to get rid of these three before they killed him. But then he was the King of Colorado. When everyone had eaten, he stood up and pointed to the door.

"The Games are over," he said, and the girls each came by, kissed him, and petted his limp and sagging manly tool, then they giggled and ran out the door as naked as they had arrived.

Klingman sat on the bed as his dresser came in with his clothes.

"Short time for the Games this week," she said.

"I was tired," he said in defense, although he seldom argued with his dresser.

"Probably. But I remember a year ago the Games lasted for a full four hours. Six times you managed it, the girls told me, although they could have been exaggerating just to show their own powers of persuasion."

"Woman, get the hell out of here," King Jacob said. One of these days he was going to have her head chopped off. He lingered as he dressed thinking about that. He'd never had one of his subject's head chopped off. It was a public punishment he could look forward to.

Klingman went to his balcony on the second floor and stood for a moment overlooking his kingdom. For as far as he could see, he controlled everything and everyone. Nobody was ever going to push him around again. Nobody.

He sat down in the chair and stared into the mists of the mountains to the north. It was cold up there, even in summer. Cold like a Texas winter night.

Texas and the damned Comanche.

An arrow slanted in from the left missing his leg by inches.

"To the left! Squads One and Two, put your fire to the left. We've got a whole damn regiment of the bastards coming at us. Now to the right. Fire at will. Cut down the fucking Comanches."

Colonel Klingman lifted his own Spencer and fired three times, blasting three Comanches off their charging war ponies.

Only they wouldn't stay dead!

The three Comanches got up and rushed ahead at him, dragging their dead bodies, heads shot off, legs missing, arms bloody. They kept coming, crawling, screaming their Comanche war cries. The filthy dead Comanches were turning the high Texas plains red with their blood.

Thousands of them, all dead and dying, rushing across the plains with their war axes poised, their bloody knives ready, fresh army scalps hanging from their horses' surcingles. All the savages bellowing for more white-eye blood.

The bastards couldn't be killed.

They were devil Indians who knew only how to fight and die and kill and rise and kill again.

Colonel Klingman's head hurt.

He held it and felt the Comanche lance penetrate his chest and tear through his heart and come out his back. Then he was one of the millions of red men struggling along the plains, charging at columns of blue soldiers, walking and riding. He was one of the bloody, ragged, screaming horde of nondead littering the Texas plains as the cavalry in new bright-blue uniforms on well-fed army mounts trotted by without looking right or left. How could they do that?

Where were the army dead?

Why did the army dead become mixed in with the Indian dead and dying?

Then he saw the battlefield at Crooked Creek.

It was still. The guns had been silenced, the bugle calls made, the Indians dashed away. Only the dying cried out for help. All else was silent. No ambulance wagon. No surgeon along. A troop this big should have a surgeon along to save the troopers. Where the hell was the doctor?

The ghosts of the army dead stood slowly and lifted into the air over his head. Some of them waved. One tried to hit Colonel Klingman as he drifted past him. Many shouted with voices that couldn't be heard except by the other dead.

The Indians came back, sweeping through the battlefield, gathering up their own dead. It was bad medicine not to take the tribe's dead away and bury them properly so their spirits could ascend into heaven.

More Indians came. The bodies of the army dead were mutilated, hacked and cut, and torn, hair taken, faces slashed, eyes gouged out so the spirits of the white-eye dead would have a harder time fighting the Comanche spirits if they ever met again in battle in the afterlife.

Colonel Jacob G. Klingman, United States Army, retired, saw the hordes of screaming, painted Comanche spilling across their lines again. He sat in the chair and relived the terrible defeat his men suffered at the

Crooked Creek fight. Tears ran down his cheeks. The King of Colorado wept bitterly until his tears wiped away all traces of the dead soldiers in front of him and washed away every sight of a Comanche and their horses, until the tears flooded away every thought of the humiliating defeat at Crooked Creek. It had cost him eighty-five of his men, his sanity, his quick shipment to Omaha, and his even quicker forced retirement for the good of the service.

Colonel Klingman, the King of Colorado, wept.

9

With the new morning, Canyon O'Grady had risen early and rode Cormac down the valley toward the far farms. He tethered the stallion palomino in the heavy brush opposite the Cuzick farm and walked through the morning dew before most of the farm families were up. He slipped into the Cuzick kitchen and found the woman of the house starting a fire.

"We were worried about you, Mr. O'Grady," she said. She wore a thin blue shirt over her nightgown and was self-conscious.

Canyon pretended not to notice. "I've been meeting people, learning a great deal. I even talked for a while with Princess Melissa."

Mrs. Cuzick looked up startled. "That's a hanging crime in this kingdom."

"So she told me. She's heartsick about what her father is doing here. She's going to help us."

"You really talked to Melissa?"

"Yes. I saw her on the back balcony of the palace and waved at her and she came out and talked to me. She was curious who had so much nerve, I imagine. She really is quite a nice person."

Cuzick himself came out of the bedroom, pulling up the suspenders on his overalls. "Thought I heard a strange voice." He knuckled sleep from his eyes. "So you're still alive."

"Mostly. I've learned Klingman has only the twenty rifles his Royal Guards use. He also has the weapons he took away from all these good people two years ago, but many of them might not be working well by now.''

"If we can get those twenty Henry rifles—'' Cuzick began.

"Better yet, I'm going to disable them, so they can't fire without a lot of gunsmith work.''

"Then a pitchfork is a damn good weapon against their clubs,'' Cuzick said, grinning.

"Now all I have to figure out is how and when,'' Canyon said. He warmed his hands near the small stove.

Two more of the group—not actually family members but quartered in the same house—got up and came into the kitchen. Then Ella came in, her hair a mess, her blouse only half-buttoned. When she saw Canyon, she did an about-face and went out of the big kitchen. Her mother grinned and shot a glance at O'Grady, who had looked away.

"So how do we get a revolution going once you're ready?'' Cuzick asked.

"For starters, we can capture and lock up all of the supervisors we can find. Colonel Daniel uses them as part of his army. But five or six to one, a supervisor's club isn't much of a stopper.''

Cuzick beamed. "Be more than glad to take care of that Waldron myself. I owe him a few licks. I'll use a three-tined pitchfork and knock that silly club of his into the next territory.''

"But not until you get the signal,'' Canyon cautioned.

"What's the signal?''

"Damn, I don't know yet. I just wanted you to know that I'm making progress. Last night I stole two kegs of black powder from the palace.''

"How in hell did you do that?'' Cuzick asked.

"Melissa has one of the guards on her bribe list and he's helping us now.''

Breakfast came for the four men. Eggs over easy, toast, jam, coffee, and fresh-fried potatoes smothered in onions. Canyon hadn't eaten so much since he left Washington.

When they finished eating, the men walked outside and leaned against the farmhouse in the shade. The other two men were in their twenties and both said they had been heading for the gold mines when their stage was taken. They said they were ready to do anything they could in the rebellion.

"You ever use a team of six horses around here?" O'Grady asked.

"No, but we use four sometimes," one of the men replied.

"The day of the rebellion I want you to have four horses here. Get ones that you can ride, if possible. That way, one of you men can ride around and alert the other farm groups that we're ready to blow the king off his throne."

Cuzick grinned. "I'm liking this more all the time. How long do we have?"

"It will be within the next two or three days. The king is getting ready to send an invasion force to capture Fort Collins. We might strike before his men can leave, or let him split his forces and hit them in two places."

"Anything we can do, just tell us," Cuzick said. "I'm tired of this pasture prison."

The other men nodded in agreement.

"I'll remember. Now, I better get moving. Thank your lady for the breakfast."

"I'll do that. Oh, I saw Waldron late yesterday. Seems he's looking for a stranger with what he called flame-red hair. Must be you. Said this person was acting funny in town."

Canyon grinned. "I ran into him. Made up a story fast and then I acted a little goofy. Guess he remembered. Thanks. I'll keep my hat on solid for a while.

I'll go down by the creek and pick up the Henry and my rounds. You folks take care of yourselves. This nightmare could be over in two or three days.''

O'Grady waved and headed for the creek in back of the house. He remembered exactly where he hid the long package wrapped so it wouldn't get wet in the dew. He came to the creek and worked up along the bank to the big oak. Just beyond it there was a little shelf of rock.

Canyon froze; his hand darted down, drew iron, and leveled it at the noise just ahead. He edged around the oak. Then he grinned.

Ella sat beside the creek, her blouse unbuttoned and the Henry rifle and the pouch of cartridges in her lap.

''Missed you at breakfast,'' she said. Her hair was brushed until it shone, her face scrubbed clean, her blouse billowing open until he could see the surging sides of both of her breasts. ''Figured you'd be coming by for your rifle,'' she said.

Canyon holstered his iron and sat down beside her. ''You figured right, pretty girl.''

She leaned over and kissed him, long and demanding.

He broke off the embrace and touched her breasts through the cloth. ''Pretty lady, I'd love to rip your clothes off right here and play sex games with you all morning until we both were exhausted, but right now I can't. I have to see a lot of people today and figure out how to topple a king from his throne.''

''I don't care, I want you to do me right now.'' She slid out of the blouse and her breasts swayed and bounced, nipples standing tall and her areolae growing a darker shade of pink by the second.

He bent and kissed one breast, then swept up the Henry and the bag of rounds. ''Darling, sweet girl, I can't just now. But I'll be back and we'll have all night, I promise.''

''One more kiss,'' she said.

Canyon bent and kissed her lips and then stepped back. "You take care of yourself and don't tangle with Waldron. I want him myself when the showdown comes." He turned and walked away through the brush along the creek toward the wooded hills at the edge of the valley where he had hidden Cormac.

He looked back once. Ella stood on her knees and now he saw she wore nothing at all. One hand caressed her own breasts. O'Grady grinned and hurried to find Cormac. He had a lot of work to do.

Canyon rode through the woods until he was at the near end of the village, then he moved another five hundred yards to the business district. He was impressed again how well it was laid out. Someone in that first commune knew what he was doing.

The agent hid Cormac in some mountain mahogany brush and worked down to where he could gather a few pinecones and walk with them into the village. He wore his hat pulled low to cover his red hair and wore the standard blue work shirt most of the people used. He figured they must be made by someone in one of the village shops.

He saw a bakery and smelled the wonderful aroma coming from it; he stopped in.

A woman behind a small counter looked up with no interest and little enthusiasm. "Yes, sir, bread for a family or for one?"

"Oh, just for one. You have any cinnamon rolls?"

The woman looked at him as if he were crazy and pushed a loaf of bread into a square of paper and wrapped it, handing it to him so his hands held the paper together. She lifted her brows at him and then vanished through a curtain that covered a door to the back. No charge for things here. That would change soon enough.

O'Grady stepped around the counter and walked past the curtain into the back room and stopped. Three men looked up at him from their positions on a bakery counter. Each was making a different kind of loaf or roll of some sort.

"You're not allowed back here," the closest man said.

"I need to talk to someone," Canyon replied.

The baker came over wiping his hands on his white uniform.

Canyon spoke softly so only this man could hear. "Would you like to be free again? Like to be able to stay here or go to Denver or wherever?"

"You from the guards or the colonel?" the baker asked.

"I'm from the outside and I'm looking for a few good men to help me with a project I have."

"The Royal Guards don't know you're in our kingdom, I'd guess?"

"If they did, I'd be the next one on the twenty-five-lash whipping post."

The man shook his head. "Not me, friend. You want to plot a revolt, you find somebody else. I got a wife and four kids. I was one of the first ones here, but old Klingman has gone crazy. I'll just wait it out. You better get out of here right now. One of our men is loyal to the king. Says he's next in line to become one of the Royal Guards. Now get moving."

O'Grady talked with three more men in the next half-hour as he wandered the town. He got much the same response from each one. Good idea, but not for him. He came out of the blacksmith's hot shed and looked up and down the street. There weren't a lot of men to talk to. Everyone seemed to be busy doing some job he had been assigned.

Down the street half a block he saw a man turn the corner. He wore the red hat of a supervisor.

The man called. "Hey, you. I want to talk to you."

Canyon put leather to street and darted between two buildings and down half a block and over another one and then around the next block. He caught his breath behind the livery stable.

He had lost the supervisor. As Canyon's breathing returned to normal, he watched a small show in the big corral behind the stables. One man was appraising twenty horses. They were all riding mounts, not plow horses. The man went from one to another, rejecting one here and there. When he threw out one, a replacement was walked in.

At last the man looked at the head wrangler. The tall man took off a light jacket and gave it back to the stable man. Now O'Grady saw the red jacket and cap of the Royal Guards. This man was the colonel himself, the defense commander and the guard chief. Evidently he had just finished picking out the twenty horses that his men would ride on the attack.

O'Grady slipped away unseen. He'd been thinking about that attack. Maybe he should let the ten Royal Guards ride off with the ten volunteers. That would split the force and get Colonel Daniel out of the way for the rebellion. Or perhaps he could confront the colonel in another area.

The cowboys. They were mounted. Had to be. He wondered about the usual free-and-easy, fiddle-footed style of a normal cowboy. How did they get this bunch tied down so easily? Would they go for a little freedom? Maybe he should ride out there soon and find out. That would be a great little surprise for the colonel on the start of his mission.

Canyon slid to the outside again, wandered into the woods as if picking berries, and vanished. Five minutes later he flashed his pocket mirror at the windows of the princess. Nothing happened. He waited ten minutes and tried it again. This time Melissa came on the balcony combing her long blond hair.

He looked for guards behind the palace and soon found only one. He was wedged into a small spot about in the center of the structure where he would be hard to see. The man didn't move for five minutes and O'Grady guessed he was sleeping. Some of these guards didn't take their jobs overly serious.

Melissa came around the side of the palace. She looked along the back of the building until she saw the guard in his small slot. She waved at him and he waved back. So he wasn't sleeping. She went toward the woods, stooped, and picked some flowers, then she found some more closer to the brush. The next few put her behind the brush; the guard didn't move.

She waited there and O'Grady walked silently to her. She jumped when he stepped out from behind a big fir tree three feet from her. "I don't see how you do that. Suddenly you're here." She smiled. "I'm glad to see that you're well. There's been some trouble in the kingdom."

"I know. I'm the cause of most of it. I hope you don't mind?"

"Not if it will help end this terrible situation. I'm sick to death of it, Mr. O'Grady."

"It soon should be over. I do need to talk to Robert again. Can you have him meet me here just at first dark?"

"I can do that." She hesitated and looked up. "I've—I've done a lot of thinking about the last time we were—the last time we touched. I know now that I shouldn't have done that, and I apologize. It's just that I don't have any experience with men. What we did, what you did, was so deliciously exciting."

"It was exciting for me as well," Canyon said. "When a man and a woman have strong feelings, it's the most wonderful experience in the world."

"Would it be too much . . ." She stopped and looked away. "I'm not good at this at all. Now if Mother had lived, she would have helped me. I should ask some other women." She sighed.

"Melissa, would it be too much if I asked if I could kiss you again?"

She looked up, her light-blue eyes sparkling, a delightful smile wreathing her face. "You're nice and thoughtful. You knew that's what I was going to say."

"It did cross my mind." He stepped closer to Princess Melissa and she lifted her beautiful face to his.

10

Canyon kissed Melissa gently on the lips and she touched his chest with her hands and then leaned back, smiling.

"Yes, oh, yes, I wasn't just dreaming." Her eyes were wide, her expression of rapture and surprise mixed with delight. "Please, please kiss me once more."

This time he pressed harder and she came to him, her chest firmly against his and her arms around him. He let her hold the kiss as long as she wished. At last she leaned back and their lips parted.

Melissa gave a long, contented sigh. "I think I've been missing a lot these last two years. I'd like to stay right here with your arms around me . . . forever."

He bent and kissed her cheek and then her nose and straightened. "It would be nice, wouldn't it? But we have other things to do that are important as well. Actions that will be important in freeing you and the people of the village."

She frowned. "Yes, of course. I—I just forgot about them for a minute. It was such a wonderful few seconds."

"You can tell Robert to be here at dusk?"

"Yes. He's still my friend and the lieutenant hasn't found out about it yet. I'll tell him as soon as I go back with my wildflowers."

As they spoke, Canyon saw a man in a red hat and

red jacket come around the corner of the palace and look toward the woods.

"Isn't that our friend there now, Colonel Daniel?"

Melissa looked and took a quick breath. "Oh, dear! He's looking for me. He says I never should be in these woods alone. I tell him he's an old fussbudget. I think he'd like to kiss me, and more, the way he looks at me sometimes. But he's never touched me."

"You better go. Take your flowers and pick some more and back out of the woods so it seems you don't know he's there. Then be casual and gentle about it."

She nodded and reached up, and he kissed her again. She melted against him, then roused, smiled an impish, cute little smile, and hurried away from him.

He watched from behind a tree as she backed out of the woods, gathering flowers and dry plants for an arrangement as she went. Colonel Daniel called to her. "Princess, your father told you not to be out here alone. I'll gladly send one of my guards with you to pick flowers."

"We did that once, Colonel, and the other guards teased him for two weeks, remember?"

"They will do what I tell them to do." The colonel made a quick motion with his hand and five guards left the far side of the palace wall and hurried to the woods.

The princess walked back toward the colonel and he motioned to the other side and five more guards from the near side of the palace ran to the edge of the woods. All ten had their rifles, but the bayonets were not mounted.

O'Grady snorted. The bastard was trying to surround him, box him in. The colonel must suspect she went to the woods to see someone. Slowly, without a sound, Canyon moved straight away from the scene and into the deeper woods. When he was fifty feet in, he paused and looked back. The ten guards worked noisily into the brush and woods, calling to one another. They penetrated the woods and brush for twenty yards and on a command all moved slowly forward.

Their sweep found nothing.

Colonel Daniel stood near the far end of the line with a puzzled look. He stared into the deeper growth for a moment and shrugged. He sent the men back to the castle and stepped behind a tall fir to wait. The colonel's back was to Canyon. The big Irishman grinned and picked up an egg-sized rock and threw it. He stepped behind a tree and out of sight as the rock hit.

Colonel Daniel grunted in surprise. The missile struck near his left foot, and he jumped and turned around. There was no indication where the rock had come from. Canyon peered through some leaves at the colonel and saw his face turn red as he pulled out his six-gun and took a step to the rear.

Then Colonel Daniels changed his mind and walked to the right. Again he paused. He had no idea where the rock had come from, except straight in back of where he had stood.

With a sudden burst of energy, the colonel ran directly to the rear into the denser brush. He ran straight for where Canyon hid for ten yards, then slowed and stopped. He was still thirty feet away through the trees and brush.

"Bastard," he spat toward the forest. "I know someone is out there. I might not find you this time, but I will soon enough. I'll find you and pull your fingernails off and tie you down on a hill of ants and then I'll cut your eyelids off and watch you go blind in the blazing sun. You'll be screaming for me to kill you quickly before it's over. You bastard!"

He turned away and Canyon found a clear path through the trees and threw another egg-sized rock. This one hit the guard in the back, and he spun around and fired. The moment he started to turn, Canyon pushed behind the big fir tree and the bullet sailed harmlessly by.

A peek around the other side of the tree showed Colonel Daniel with the revolver out ready to shoot again. His face was fire-red now, his nostrils flaring, mouth open sucking in air.

"Bastard," the colonel shouted again and ran straight ahead at full speed. He headed for the best concealment in the area, the Douglas fir tree Canyon hid behind.

The government agent had time only to draw his pistol and hold it high as the colonel thundered forward, crashing brush and small trees as he charged for the fir.

Just as he came to it, Canyon swung his heavy pistol downward. The pistol handle and the colonel's red cap met in a dead heat. The colonel's eyes rolled up and he fell the other direction, slipping into unconsciousness before he slammed into the forest floor.

Canyon stood for a moment with his revolver centered on the colonel's head. The man didn't move. Slowly O'Grady bent and picked up the revolver that had fallen from the man's hand. It was an unusual weapon.

Canyon stared at it for a minute before he saw the difference. There were no nipples on the cylinders. It was one of the rare breech-loading revolvers. A true metal-cartridge revolver. The name came to him, Smith & Wesson revolver #2. They were first made in 1857 and he had tried to get one.

O'Grady found a pouch on the officer's belt that contained more than two dozen metal rounds for the weapon. It was a small bore, maybe a .38 or a .32. But up close, it would be effective and could be reloaded rapidly.

He pushed the cartridge pouch inside his shirt and stuffed the small revolver in his waist band. As a lark, he tied the man's hands behind his back with stout leather thong from his pocket, then Canyon slipped off into the brush toward the spot where he had left Cormac. He knew the ten guards had heard the pistol shot and would soon come back to check on their leader.

He rode higher on the slope so he could see the whole valley. It was a beautiful spot. Soon he hoped that it would be as free as it was attractive.

Tonight he would go back to the Cuzick farm, he thought. He might have the start of an organized group going.

It was three or four hours to dusk. Canyon stepped down from Cormac and patted the big stallion on the neck. ''Cormac, lad, I think we'll take a bit of a rest now. Get in some snooze before the work tonight.''

He ground-tied the animal and kicked free some sticks from a splotch of grass and lay down. Soon he was sleeping and dreaming of Ireland and its remarkable green on green.

Canyon awoke as Cormac made low sounds in his throat. The agent was up at once, his army revolver in his hand. The horse looked downhill and to the left.

O'Grady cupped Cormac's nostrils a moment so he wouldn't make any more sounds as he looked downhill. Through the brush fifty yards away he saw three men afoot, beating the trees and shrubs as they worked uphill. They came another ten yards, then sat down and talked quietly.

Now and then one would whack a stick against a tree and they would shout to one another as if conducting a search. A few minutes later the men stood and began working back down through the brush on another angle toward the village.

''Cormac, it looks like Colonel Daniel is really upset. We might have picked the wrong spot for a meeting with Robert.''

The sun was nearly down behind the peaks to the west. It made sundown come early, but darkness much later. Canyon led the stallion down the slope, adjusting to the left, pausing regularly to listen for anyone searching the brush. It seemed clear.

He left Cormac fifty yards up the hill and moved down without a sound to the big fir he had used before as a lookout spot. He could see the castle through the fringes of trees and brush.

Just before dusk, he saw a figure slip from the far wall and glide into the forest. He couldn't be sure who it was. He watched for another few minutes but saw no one else following the first man. So far, so good.

A short time later he saw Robert come into the brush below him. He squatted and watched. The man moved fairly well in the woods. O'Grady made the sound of a mourning dove and Robert looked around. Canyon moved into plain sight and motioned, and the guard worked up the hill to the big fir.

"Thought I missed you," Robert said. "We had a hell of a lot of excitement around here. I figured maybe the colonel caught you, but then he came back so mad he couldn't even talk. I noticed that his prize possession, his solid-cartridge revolver, was gone from his holster."

"You mean this little Smith and Wesson Number Two?" Canyon held it up and Robert laughed softly.

"Damn, you're one hell of a man to take that away from the colonel him with ten men backing him."

"Not a big problem. How is the armory? Can we get in there tonight?"

"Probably. I hear there will be two men on guard. Both with loaded weapons. That's unusual."

"Can we get to them and get inside? I'll need about half an hour with those rifles."

"Shouldn't be any problem. We'll go in the middle of their four-hour shift. First watch starts at six tonight."

"So, if we hit them about midnight, they'll be getting a little tired and sleepy?"

"Indeed they will. That's the toughest tour."

"Tell me what room the armory is in, just in case anything goes wrong."

"By God, nothing better go wrong, or it's my neck. I know, I've seen the colonel operate before, and he's bare-assed furious tonight. This could really set him off."

"We hope he'll never know we've been there. That's the whole idea."

"Let's hope so." Robert wiped sweat from his forehead even though it wasn't that hot. "Remember where we were for the powder? Instead of going down those steps, we go along that closest hall. The armory is the first door. It's always locked and there'll be two men outside it, armed and waiting. How the hell do we get past them?"

"You'll know them? Know their names?"

"Sure, I know all the guys in the Royal Guards."

"Good. That'll be enough. There'll be a man on the front door, right?"

"As usual."

"We'll get him the way we did before so he doesn't identify you. If one of these guys makes out who you are, you'll be coming with me for your own protection. In two days more and the revolution will be here."

"Let's hope."

At midnight they walked up to the front door of the castle and knocked. The guard cracked the door an inch and both men slammed into it with their shoulders. It floored the guard inside, but not before he saw Robert. They tied and gagged the man and dragged him to the side. He carried a percussion revolver, but it wasn't loaded.

Robert pushed it in his belt and hurried up the steps and around the corner to the first hallway. He pulled Canyon along behind him as if he had a prisoner.

"Hey, men," Robert shouted, "look who I caught.

That damn red-haired giant we've been hearing about."

The two Royal Guards on duty at the armory door looked up and grinned.

"How did you do it, Robert? Looks like he could break you in half."

"All in knowing what you're doing," Robert said. By then they were within three feet of the Royal Guards. Robert let go of Canyon and both men slammed fists, knees, and elbows into the two guards. They went down from shock and surprise. Canyon and Robert tied them up and gagged them.

Robert took one of the men's caps and his rifle and dragged the two groggy guards into the armory. Canyon blindfolded the guards so they couldn't see what he was doing as Robert stood watch outside.

O'Grady struck a stinker match and soon found a lamp, which he lit. The Henry rifles were neatly set in a rack along the wall. He searched the room and found a small hammer and a long screwdriver.

With these he worked over the Henry rifles, quickly opening the breech and breaking off the tip of the firing pin in each of the weapons. He returned each one to the rack and then started to trade one for the weapon Robert held. He changed his mind. He counted. Eighteen. The one Robert had was nineteen. There would be one rifle that could fire, but he had no idea where it was.

He slipped outside.

Robert grinned. "I guess I'm with you now whether I want to be or not. Let's get moving."

"That weapon loaded?" Canyon asked. Robert nodded. "Good, you keep that as your own rifle. We might need some more firepower later."

They hurried outside with Robert carrying the weapon ready to fire in case they ran into any trouble.

The two revolutionaries slipped around the palace and into the woods without being stopped.

When they got to Cormac, Robert looked up in amazement at the big stallion. "I've heard about this horse, but almost nobody has seen him. What a beauty!"

Canyon mounted and took his boot out of the left-hand stirrup. "Step in there and mount up behind me. Cormac is good at carrying two men. We're like a pair of roosters on his big back. We'll ride out to the farms and sleep the rest of the night in some brush along a creek and have a fine breakfast in the morning," Canyon said as Robert hopped atop the sturdy horse. "How do you like being a traitor, a robber, a revolutionary, and a free man so far?"

Robert grinned. "Damn, I like it better than anything I've done in the past two years. This is great!"

11

With first light the next morning, O'Grady was sitting by the creek watching the world come alive. A red-headed woodpecker flew in and shrieked at Canyon for being in his well-defined territory.

Robert stirred, rolled over on the soft ground and mulch under the trees. Suddenly he sat up alarmed, wide-eyed.

"What the hell? Oh—oh, yeah. O'Grady and the great revolution."

"Welcome to the morning. I thought you might sleep until noon. Hungry?"

"Starving. What do I eat, crawdads and milkweed?"

"If you want to. Otherwise I'm sure the Cuzicks would share a bit of their breakfast with us. Right over that way."

Robert looked through the brush and spotted the farmhouse.

"Why didn't you say so? Can you wait until I get my boots on?"

As the two of them walked up to the farmhouse, Canyon took off his hat so his red hair would identify him. A moment later Ella came bursting out the door and ran to meet them. She slowed a few steps away.

"Ella, what a fine welcome. This is Robert. He's one of us now and will be staying with you or hiding out here in the brush for a couple of days. Your friend Mr. Waldron been around any?"

"He comes most every day. Getting bolder and bolder," she said, frowning.

"Your pa home?"

" 'Deed his is. You staying the night?"

"Aim to. Be here for most of the day. I have some business in the village for part of the evening, and then I'll come back."

"Good." She ran ahead of them, held the door open, and without anyone seeing, patted Canyon's bottom as he went into the house.

Everyone was at the breakfast table. Cuzick got up for the introduction.

"This is Robert. He's with me, he's one of us now and has helped a lot getting things started." They said their hellos all around.

"Got a surprise for you, O'Grady," Cuzick said. "I been talking to some of the other farm groups. Got four good solid men coming over here this noon for a little get-together to talk about what we'll do when the revolt starts."

Canyon frowned. "I hope you were quiet about it. Colonel Daniel is hurting to find somebody to punish."

"Hell, I'm smarter than that, O'Grady. Only talked to five men and four of them said yes. Fifth man is a good friend of mine and he said he wouldn't tell anybody else, he'd just forget I was there."

"They're coming at noon?" O'Grady asked.

"Nearabouts."

"We'll see what happens. Robert here is a new convert. He used to be one of the guards around the castle. He's helped me a lot. Be grateful if he could hide out here for a day or so."

"Damn right. More than welcome." Cuzick looked at his wife. "Woman, we got two men over here about half-starved. You gonna get some grub this way or do you need some help?"

She glared at her husband, then brought two plates

to the table. On each were four eight-inch diameter pancakes a half-inch thick with butter on top and syrup. On the side were strips of thick-cut bacon. She brought sunny-side-up eggs and served up three on each plate. Ella poured large cups of coffee.

"What's happening at the palace?" Ella asked the men. "We heard they been having some problems."

Robert kept his head down and ate.

Canyon nodded and told them about talking to the princess and how she was helping. He didn't mention the rifles. It was hard to know exactly whom you could trust.

After breakfast, Canyon and Robert spent an hour cleaning and oiling the Henry rifle that Robert carried. It had been months since it had been broken down and cleaned. Now there would be no problem with it jamming if it indeed were fired. Robert's newfound pistol was still unloaded, since the caliber must be a .45 and Canyon's linen cartridges wouldn't stay rammed in the cylinder. But just having two firearms made Robert the envy of the other men and made him stand a foot taller.

Some of the neighboring men began coming about ten that morning. As soon as someone could be seen on the trail coming in, Canyon and Robert went to the creek and built a small blind they could hide behind and yet see the farmyard plainly some fifty yards away.

Robert took a nap in a spot of sunshine with one hand trailing in the cool water of the creek.

Canyon watched the men arrive. When the fourth had come, the agent got ready to go up and talk to them. He wasn't sure what Cuzick had told them, but it would be good to have a few men on his side when the shooting started.

Cuzick came out of the house and waved both arms toward the creek. That was the signal for O'Grady to come up. Then someone shouted something and Cuzick ran to the front of the house. A moment later he returned, holding his hands up to tell Canyon to stay away.

Something was wrong.

O'Grady made sure his .44 was in its holster as he shook Robert awake.

"Get that Henry limbered up, we might need it. Cuzick just signaled that there's some problem up there. You stay here. I'll go see. Cover me."

Canyon left the blind on a run. He sprinted to the back wall and stopped, panting. He heard men talking at the front of the house. When he edged around the corner, he could see nothing out front. He went to the other corner and saw the five men standing in the yard waiting for someone who came riding down the lane.

Who would be riding a horse? The colonel? A few seconds later, O'Grady could make out the red cap of a supervisor. It was Waldron.

"Damn," Canyon muttered. This must be important. Why was Waldron riding a horse? O'Grady couldn't move any closer without showing himself. There was no back door in the house. He watched from low on the wall and listened.

"Damn, we better run," one of the newcomers said.

"No chance, he's seen all five of us. He can run us down with that horse."

"Why's he got a horse, now of all times?"

It was obvious to Canyon from the way Waldron rode that he was angry and in a rush. He pulled to a stop in front of the five men.

"Why are you all here? What is this, a revolt? Who's responsible for this unlawful gathering?"

Nobody said a word.

"I've had my eye on you, Cuzick. You've been doing too much traveling around. You're the ringleader of this revolt. I have an eyewitness and all the evidence I need. I've had permission from the colonel to handle the situation any way I please."

Waldron kicked the horse in the flanks and it jolted

forward directly at the surprised Cuzick. He had time to jump to the left to avoid the charging horse, but landed right in the way of the long hard club that Waldron swung.

The baton hit Cuzick on the shoulder, breaking his shoulder blade and bringing a wail of pain and anger from him. He staggered away, but Waldron whipped the horse around and swung the club again. It grazed down the side of Cuzick's head.

O'Grady had been caught by surprise. The baton had slammed into Cuzick twice before the special U.S. agent leapt to his feet and surged around the side of the house.

Waldron swung the club again and it hit the top of Cuzick's head and he screamed and fell to his knees.

O'Grady bellowed a challenge as he charged past the front of the house and angled for Cuzick thirty feet ahead of him.

Waldron's head snapped up and he stared at O'Grady and kicked the horse around to run it straight at him. In one swift, practiced move the agent drew the army percussion revolver from his holster, swung it up, cocking the hammer with his thumb. He pointed the big gun at the rider and fired, all in one motion and so quick that Waldron never had a chance to dodge.

The heavy .44-caliber ball hit Waldron in his right shoulder, smashing into the joint, splattering as it came to the bones, digging a dozen holes through flesh, and burying in bone and tendon.

Waldron spun off the mount, dropped his baton, and fell on his good shoulder, rolling in the dust. The horse slowed and stopped.

Waldron lay in the dust a moment, then pushed upright with his left arm until he was in a sitting position.

"Bastard," Waldron screamed. "You shot me."

Canyon O'Grady ignored the downed supervisor. He had lost his red hat, his badge of authority. Canyon rushed past him to where Cuzick knelt on the ground. Gently O'Grady helped the farmer sit down. The top and the side of his face were bloody, his eyes were closing and opening.

"Cuzick, hang on. You're going to be all right. Hang on, Cuzick." He motioned for two of the men who stood nearby shocked. "You and you. Get over here and carry Cuzick into the shade."

The men came and knelt beside their friend.

Canyon stood and turned toward Waldron. The supervisor had tried to stand, but didn't quite make it. He dropped back down to his knees, then sat on the ground. He stared up at O'Grady as he came up to him.

"Who the hell are you?"

"If Cuzick dies, I'm your executioner." Canyon's boot lashed out and caught Waldron beside the head and tumbled him over on his shot shoulder. Waldron roared in pain. Canyon picked up Waldron's club, well-painted and -polished, with a leather thong through one end. He carried it to Waldron and tapped him on the head with it.

The supervisor looked up now, fear in his eyes. "Just doing my job," Waldron said. "Christ, I'm just doing what I'm told to do."

"And your job is intimidating, beating, and killing people. You do your job well. Strange coincidence. I've got the same job and I'm just doing my job." O'Grady brought the club back as if to strike Waldron, but swung it over the man's head, missing him by inches.

Canyon's boot toe stabbed an inch into the supervisor's side. "Waldron, you stay right there. You move so much as six inches and I'll blow your brains out where you crawl."

He hurried back to Cuzick. The men hadn't moved him. He lay now in the shade the two men made with their bodies. One of the men shook his head slowly.

O'Grady knelt by Cuzick. His eyes came open for a moment and his stare locked on Canyon. "We gave them a run, O'Grady. We had them worried. Finish it. Sorry I can't help. Finish it for all of us."

Cuzick nodded slowly, then his eyes stared at eternity and his head fell lifeless to the side. Canyon reached out and closed his eyelids, then nodded at the men and motioned for them to take him into the farmhouse.

O'Grady turned back to where Waldron sat in the dirt. The agent took his six-gun and pushed the muzzle in Waldron's mouth.

"Today, Waldron, you beat to death with a club an unarmed, nonviolent man. You must be proud. You must think of yourself as a real hero. You'll remember beating Cuzick to death for the rest of your life, since your earthly existence isn't going to last more than five minutes. You understand me?"

The six-gun barrel twisted in Waldron's mouth, and his eyes flared in pain. He looked at O'Grady, his eyes pleading.

"I'm going to take this weapon out of your mouth and then I'm going to ask you some questions. You better answer them fast and completely, or I'll start shooting you in the knees and then your elbows and then your balls. You understand?" He removed the gun.

"Yes, sir," Waldron whispered.

"Fine. How many Henry rifles does Colonel Daniel have?"

"Twenty, and about twenty more old civilian rifles and shotguns."

"Where are the civilian arms?"

"In the same place the Henry rifles are."

"How many men can he raise to fight?"

"Forty. The Royal Guards, the House Guards, and ten or fifteen supervisors."

"What is the colonel doing today?"

"I don't know."

"Why did you kill Cuzick?"

"He had been talking to the other farmers about a revolt."

"Do you want to die?"

"No."

"You're going to. Now stand up and start walking."

"I can't."

"Then you die right here. Want to try to walk?"

Waldron struggled to stand. He held his right arm across his chest with his left hand. He moved slowly, carefully, gritting his teeth with each step.

"Back up the road toward town. No sense making the rest of the people here suffer anymore."

O'Grady looked back at the men near the porch. "Gentlemen, the meeting is over. The revolt will begin tomorrow or the next day. Now go home and get ready." He poked Waldron in the back with his six-gun. "Move it, killer. You've got a date with death right down the road."

O'Grady wasn't happy with the situation. He wasn't an executioner, although this man deserved it if any man ever did. He wasn't about to hang him properly. He didn't want to blow the man's skull off in front of the women and the others back there. That would prove he wasn't much better than their present overlords.

The bastard would make a try along here somewhere. O'Grady might even have to give him a chance.

A quarter of a mile down the road the stream that ran past the Cuzick house crossed the lane.

"Get over here, I want a drink." Canyon waited while Waldron walked into the shade, then he bent down just below the man and started to drink. He saw the bulk coming at him. Waldron was throwing himself down on top of his tormentor.

Just before Waldron hit him, O'Grady turned and fired one round into the man's snarling face.

The force of the .44 round blew Waldron over two

feet, and he fell half in the stream beside the agent. There was no reason to check to see if the man was dead. The top half of his skull had sprayed out in a hundred pieces as the slug tore out of his head.

O'Grady left the dead man where he lay. The U.S. agent got up and walked back to the house, reloading the two spent rounds as he walked. He took linen cartridges from the small pouch on his belt, inserted them in the fired cylinders, and pushed them home solidly with the small ramrod. Then he put fresh detonation caps on the nipples and crimped them in place. He settled the .44 in leather, fastened the hold-down strap, and walked on down the road toward the Cuzick home to pay his respects to the dead and his condolences to Ella and to the widow.

12

Colonel Daniel had found only two men with previous military experience as he rode up and down the village that morning. He drafted them into service and then began selecting the eight others he would need. He stared down at a man from the blacksmith shop. He was slender and strong.

The colonel knew the man had a wife and two children. "Johnson, can you ride a horse?"

"Done some riding, Colonel."

"Ever shot a rifle?"

"Of course, back before. Always brought meat home."

"Good you're reassigned to the cavalry. Step out here and go with the sergeant."

"I didn't volunteer, Colonel," the smithy said.

Anger flared in the colonel. His lean face, with its hook nose, flushed and his deep-set eyes took on an anger the smithy could feel.

"Johnson, you are assigned to this new job. If you fail to function in it adequately, there will be certain requirements made of your pretty wife by some of my troops. Do I make myself plain, Johnson, or do you want me to spell things out in much greater detail?"

Now anger touched the tall blacksmith's face, but he controlled it. He nodded slowly. "Yes, sir, Colonel. I'll be in your cavalry."

It took Colonel Daniel half the morning to find the

ten men. He had to offer veiled threats to get the co-operation of most of them.

Now he had them all behind the livery stable. Each man was given a saddle, had the stirrups adjusted for height, and a boot attached that would hold a Henry rifle.

The colonel had been outraged that morning when he learned that one of his House Guards had assaulted some of the Royal Guards and tied them up and evidently gone into the armory. Only one of the Henry rifles was missing. He couldn't figure it out. If a man had wanted to escape why wouldn't he take several of the rifles?

The colonel himself had looked over the weapons and saw nothing wrong with them. He didn't fire any because ammunition was scarce. It was a mystery he would have to live with. The guards assaulted and tied up proved not to be injured seriously and were back on duty. Nothing could be allowed to slow the conquest of Fort Collins, the colonel thought.

Colonel Daniel had served in the U.S. Army Cavalry. He knew what men could do on horseback and what was expected. These men who had little riding experience would do fine. All they had to do for now was sit on the saddle and not fall off. It would be much like new recruits in the cavalry. The army sent them directly to units with no training. Any training the new men got had to be done by the units, and often there wasn't time. He had seen more than one cavalry trooper fall off his horse and not be able to get back on.

They made a three-mile ride up the valley and back. While the men were still lined up, the colonel addressed them.

"Men, you'll stay in the barracks tonight. We'll leave in the morning for a ride to Fort Collins, where we will attack and subjugate the local population, establishing a new province of the kingdom.

"The day before we reach Fort Collins you will be given instruction in loading and firing the Henry repeating rifle you will be issued. You ten men will be bolstered by ten of my regular Royal Guards. There may be some fighting, but it will be minimal.

"For the next two hours you will learn how to saddle and care for your horse. I'll see you again bright and early in the morning."

The colonel rode away and the sergeant working with him began the instruction in how to handle a horse, how to mount and dismount, how to take off a saddle and then how to put on the saddle.

The colonel hurried back to his quarters in the first floor of the palace. Marie was waiting for him and he was determined to wear her out before he left. He thought about last night and nearly fell down. What a night that had been! This was one of the great little benefits of working for a king: he had all the women he wanted, all the time.

He might kill himself with some young wench someday, but what a way to die! Right now he had all afternoon and half the night to play and devise new positions. When he started getting tired himself, he'd put her on top and make her do the work. The colonel grinned and ran up the steps and into the palace.

Back at the Cuzick ranch, the men had taken turns digging the long narrow grave. They went down five feet in the rich soil and then walked slowly to the house.

When the widow saw Canyon, she flew at him, her small fists pounding against his chest until she gave up and sobbed and let him put his arms around her.

O'Grady knew her anger. If he had never stopped at their ranch that first day, her husband would still be alive. When the widow calmed down, he asked her if she was ready. She shuddered as she took a deep breath, wiped her eyes, and nodded.

Canyon led her out to the grave where the other men had carried the body. She went to it and opened the flap of blanket over her husband's face and stared at it a long time, then kissed his cheek.

The four men put the body on ropes and lowered the mortal remains of Cuzick into the hole. That was when O'Grady realized that he had never known the man's first name.

"I want a service," the widow said softly.

One of the visiting ranchers had been a Baptist minister for a time, and he said the words and made the promises of eternal life and how they would all meet again in Beulah land. Then the widow dropped in a handful of dirt, dry-eyed now but still angry.

She pushed the men away and took a shovel and began crying again as she shoveled all the dirt back into the hole, watching as each shovelfull she dropped in covered up her husband a little more until the blanket was gone from sight and so was her husband and half of her life.

She screeched at anyone who touched a shovel. She worked steadily for an hour putting all the dirt back in the hole. Then she tramped it down and mounded up the dirt and made a cross with David James Cuzick printed on it.

When she finished, the widow sat down beside the grave and the men couldn't persuade her to leave. O'Grady figured she would be there until darkness.

The neighbors left, swearing vengeance on the fifth man who Cuzick had talked to about the revolt. They would find him and kill him this afternoon.

Ella had made food for anyone who wanted to eat. O'Grady sat with her for a while. She had cried, then dried her tears and realized she would have to take care of her mother and somehow provide after the revolt. She had no idea how.

"You coming back tonight? You promised," she said.

"I'll be back. It may be late."

"Just come back."

Canyon nodded. It was late afternoon before he got away. He told Robert to stay near the blind and to keep Waldron's horse there in the thick brush and out of sight. It would be his after the revolt. He could ride it perhaps on the big march against the castle.

O'Grady brought with him from the farm three gallon cans and a piece of soft cotton cloth two feet square. He rode his usual route through the pines and firs, until he was to the spot where he had hidden the black powder.

He dismounted and uncovered the first keg and spent some time measuring out the powder into the three gallon cans. He tore the cotton cloth into strips and folded it carefully to use as fuses. He unfolded the cloth and sprinkled powder on it, then rolled it up and tied each end with threads from the selvage edge of the cloth. The burning cloth and the sprinkling of black powder would make a quick burning fuse for the petard.

He carried the three cans of powder, the fuses, and the half-filled keg to the edge of the woods well on the other side of the castle. On his various trips through the village, he had seen three or four unused buildings that must have once been stores but now were no longer needed. He chose one not close to any other and slipped the hasp off the back door and walked inside.

He placed the half-filled keg of black powder on the floor by the front wall. He tipped the keg on its side, then upside down so there was a trail of powder under the edge of the keg to the mother lode.

Outside, he walked around the building to make certain no one would be harmed. Back inside he took a two-foot cloth fuse he had laced with black powder, and pushed one end of it under the powder keg. Then with a stinker match he tore off a waxed bundle, he lit the fuse and raced out the back door and toward the woods at the edge of the village.

The fuse burned much faster than he thought it would, and less than fifteen seconds after he got out of the building, the night sky lit up with a tremendous explosion as the powder went off. The containment of the powder inside the keg made the force even greater.

O'Grady looked back and saw the front wall of the structure blow outward. The second story collapsed and then the roof fell in and flames licked at the dry lumber and the oiled logs. Soon the building burned with such an intensity that no amount of bucket-brigade work would even touch it.

After a few tries the dozen men who ventured out with buckets stood back and watched the flames eat away at the wreck of a building.

Quickly Colonel Daniel and six Royal Guards appeared.

"How did it happen?" the colonel asked. "Was anyone seen near this building tonight?" He got no cooperation.

So this was why the redhead had stolen the powder, the colonel thought. He was attacking the village. But not the castle. Colonel Daniel wondered why. He put his troops into a patrolling mode and strung them out along the edge of the village. The malcontent must be using he woods as his lair, the same as he did when he stole the Colonel's favorite six-gun.

"You have your rifles, men, with rounds. If you see anyone lurking in the woods or running from or to the brush along here, shoot to kill."

O'Grady knelt behind some brush in the edge of the woods in back of the village and could hear the colonel's orders. He had no desire to be shot at, but more important, he didn't want any of the guards to try to shoot and discover that his firing pin was broken. The agent crept deeper into the woods and decided to wait out the search.

Nearly two hours later Canyon used one of the gallon containers half full of powder and turned it upside down near the back of a store at the other end of the village and lit the foot-long fuse. He sprinted for the woods and just made it when the bomb went off in the open.

The crackling roar made more noise outside than the first bomb had made. But it caused no damage other than a blackened hole a foot deep into the ground.

Now Canyon took his last two bombs and fuses and went through the woods and back to the area near the palace. He checked for guards, found none behind the palace, and set both bombs against a window on the first floor. A strike closer to home would upset the Royal Guards and might make some of them quit. O'Grady lit the fuses both at once, then he hurried into the woods.

The double explosion here brought screams from the first floor, and lamps glowed in other parts of the castle. Even before the guards could find where the damage was, O'Grady was back on Cormac riding down the valley through the fringe of the woods and toward the streams and the Cuzick ranch house.

13

Canyon pulled the palomino into the brush near the blind he and Robert had made along the creek that morning. O'Grady stepped off the mount, pulled off the saddle, and put it on a rock, then he loosely tied the animal to a willow. He rubbed his ears for a moment and then walked toward the blind.

Ella met him a dozen steps later. She ran into his arms, hugged him so tight it hurt, and kissed him. When she let him go, she pulled his hand toward the house. "Ma says no sense having to rough it out here on the ground. We got a perfect good bed in the cabin and we can have the light burning and all. She says I get a better chance to get knocked up in a bed. You like it that way?"

"I do. What about you, Ella? You want the light on?"

"Figure as how. I need me a really good look at you, 'cause I'm not sure but I might be getting just a little bit pregnant. Might be last time I can really dick around with a handsome man as good as you."

"Robert here?"

"Yep. Bedded down there in the brush. I didn't bother him none. Wanted to keep my cunt fresh and ready for you." She looked up at him. "Hope you don't mind a little dirty talk. It gets me going if'n I can say them bad words a few times."

"Doesn't bother me a bit," O'Grady said, and put his hand out and fondled her firm breasts.

"Oh, Lordy, that does feel good. Feels better than when I do it to myself. Just the idea of it, I guess."

"Sometimes you rub yourself off?" he asked.

She laughed. "Sure as hell. What girl don't, in my fix? All this good body and no husband. Damn, I bet you jacked off yourself once in a while."

"No argument."

They went in the farmhouse quietly, eased across the kitchen and into the bedroom on the left. The other women were in the right-hand side room and the men slept in the barn. It had been that way for six months.

They closed the door and the girl lit a lamp. In the soft glow, she looked not only beautiful, but damn tempting. Already she had loosened her blouse so one side swung out showing a breast.

Ella sat down on the bed and motioned for him to join her. She kissed him and then eased back.

"First thing I want to do is see you all bare-assed naked. You're such a pretty man I want to feel all of them muscles and watch them work and find out where your damn balls go when your prick gets all hard. Any objections?"

"You're my hostess and I'm freeloading, what can I say?" Canyon smiled.

She slid out of her blouse and turned the lamp up. Her breasts swung as she went to the far dresser and brought over another lamp and lit it. The room brightened and she nodded.

O'Grady began to undo his shirt, but she stopped him.

"Hey, there, that's woman's work. I get to unwrap you like a birthday present and see all the goodies inside."

"You unwrapped either of them prospectors you got on the farm here? Both young bucks."

"Tried one of them. Didn't like him, he was too rough and demanding. I told him to poke his dick in one of our sows next time he got a boner, and he got mad. Won't touch either one. I want me a real man."

She stripped off his shirt and attacked his nipples, pinching them, kissing them, cupping the swell. He grabbed her breasts and pulled her down on the bed on top of him. She lifted and dropped one big breast into his mouth.

"Oh, Lordy, but that is heaven. Don't know why a man sets me on fire chewing on my titties. Sure does a job on me. I'm so hot to get poked!" She lifted away from him. "So we slow it down. You're the item here to be examined." She straddled his legs one at a time with her face toward his and pulled off his boots, and his socks.

She pulled his legs together and undid his belt, then the buttons on his fly. At last she lifted his hips and pulled down his pants and the short underwear he had on. At once she exclaimed in delight.

"He is just as big as I remembered! Lordy, what a monster. To think he found a home all the way inside my little pussy! Lordy, Lordy, but that will be glorious again." She rolled him over, patted his buttocks, and massaged his back and his flaring shoulder muscles. "Muscles all over the place. You have so many and they are all so full and heavy. Just beautiful." She turned him one way, then another on the bed, at last posed him on his hands and knees.

That was when he grabbed her and pulled off her skirt and fell hard on top of her, his mouth over one breast. He looked up and she grinned.

"I just wondered how long you could hold out all naked and ready to make love that way," she said.

"Not as long as you could, I'd wager," O'Grady said. He lifted away from her, found the magic node at her crotch, and twanged it ten times, sending her into a shouting climax that tore through her. She surged up with a bursting desire that turned her face beautiful.

"Never before . . ." she began, then stopped. "Now, right now, O'Grady, before I lose my mind. Make love to me like a devoted husband wanting to get me pregnant. Make it so damn deep I'll taste you."

He went into her pink treasure slowly, then penetrated as deeply as he could, and with short quick strokes developed a rhythm that roused him in seconds and blasted his seed deeply into her.

It was twenty minutes before they came awake from their catnap, both still locked together. He rolled away and she sat up.

"Hey, I bet you didn't have anything to eat since breakfast, right? You must be starved. I'll put on a nightgown and fix you some sandwiches. You just stay put."

He lolled on the bed as she slipped into a cotton nightgown and hurried into the kitchen. He heard voices a few minutes later and looked out. Mother and daughter were deep in conversation, then Mrs. Cuzick nodded, whispered something else, and went back into the women's bedroom.

When Ella came in the bedroom several minutes later, she had a tray with three big sandwiches made of two slices of home-made bread each and two glasses of milk.

"Milk keeps you sexy," Ella said.

He took a bite out of one of the sandwiches and realized he was indeed hungry. The first sandwich was filled with roast beef, cheese, and pickles. The second he got halfway through and figured out it was cheddar cheese and strawberry jam. What a wonderful combination. He finished the sandwich and one glass of milk.

"I'll save the rest for a snack," he said. "Didn't I hear your mother out there?"

"Sure, she was coaching me. I told her you wouldn't mind if she came in and watched, but she pretended to slap me. Her best advice was to stay on my back, the old missionary position, because that's the best way to get pregnant. She said it worked for her four times. Oh, she lost one baby, the second boy died when he was about six, and my older brother is somewhere in St. Louis. We lost track of him, since we can't write letters outside.''

"All that is going to change tomorrow," O'Grady said.

"Mean what Pa said was right? You're going to start the revolution tomorrow?"

"If it all goes the way we want it to. I'll be leaving here about two in the morning to ride out to where the cowboys have their house. I figure them being free spirits they'll want to help, and they have horses.''

"Sure, but they also have the meanest son-of-a-bitch supervisor in this whole place. I hear he hanged a cowboy out there about a year ago.''

"So we'll take care of him first. He can cooperate or taste lead. Right now I don't care which.''

"Damn I'd like to ride with you.''

"Not a chance.''

"Just because I'm a woman. I can shoot a rifle better than my pa. I ever tell you that? We used to have contests and I'd always win with the old flintlock we used to have.''

"I believe you. But how can you help populate the West if you get yourself shot up?''

"How can we populate the West if all the men get their balls shot off?''

She stared at him and then they both laughed and fell on the bed. It seemed like a short night until two in the morning. They figured out another wild way to make love, and twice more they tried to ''plant the seed'' as her mother had directed Ella.

O'Grady finished the third sandwich before he put his pants on. It was sausage and sauerkraut, one of the best sandwiches he'd ever eaten.

He finished dressing and Ella sat in his lap, naked as a newborn pup.

"You taking Robert with you?" Ella asked.

"Damn right. Two guns are better than one. We have to get through the checkpoint without losing a lot of time."

O'Grady kissed her once more, then stood, dumping her bare bottom on the bed. "I'll be back tomorrow sometime, and when I come, I want everyone ready with a weapon of some kind as we all march on the castle. The men should have pitchforks and axes, the women knives and hatchets. I'll see you tomorrow."

Canyon slipped out of the bedroom and across the kitchen. Once outside, he ran to the creek and rousted out Robert. "Rise and shine, trooper, time to march. Get your pants and boots on, we're moving."

They were in the saddle five minutes later, with Robert only partly awake. He carried the fully loaded Henry repeating rifle over his saddle and blinked at the darkness. "What the hell time is it, anyway?"

"Three-thirty A.M. You expect to sleep to noon in this federal service?"

"Well, where we going?"

When Canyon told him, he shook his head. "We won't even get through the checkpoint on the road."

O'Grady patted the rifles and pistols. "Why do you suppose we have these? I doubt if the checkpoint guards have any rounds in their weapons."

They rode down the main road that the agent had come in on only a few days ago. It amazed him that so much had happened in so little time.

They rode slowly, then walked their mounts as they came toward the checkpoint gate. It was closed and some chains were around it.

"Can you jump that horse?" Canyon asked Robert.

"No. I'm lucky to be able to stay in the saddle when she's got all four feet on the ground."

They rode forward, hoping there would be a guard. Nobody seemed to be at the gate. Both rode right up to the barrier and O'Grady bellowed in his best voice. "Hey, there, you guards. Get your asses out here, now."

One man staggered from the door, rubbing his eyes.

"You, guard. Over here. We're an advance scouting party for the Royal Guards. They're coming through tomorrow on a special mission to capture Fort Collins. Open this damn gate right now."

Another man stepped from the shadows; he was holding a Henry rifle. He did not aim it at the pair but held it so he could bring it up if he had to.

"I'm in charge here," said the man with the rifle. "I've had no word about any scouts coming through."

"Do we look like renegades? We both have Henry rifles like yours. Now open the damn gate."

"We'll wait until morning." The man started to turn away. O'Grady drew his six-gun and shot the checkpoint supervisor in the right leg, knocking him down and sending his rifle tumbling to the ground. He sat up, shocked.

"You shot me. You have live ammunition?"

"A weapon isn't much good without it. Now you, guard, get over here and open the gate or take a slug through your heart. Which one do you prefer?"

The first guard ran to the gate, undid some chains, and threw the gate open.

The two men walked their horses through. O'Grady stopped his big palomino near the shot guard. "You better get that leg tended to before you bleed to death. Next time, do as you're ordered."

Canyon and Robert turned their backs on the checkpoint guards and rode on down the track of a trail toward the next valley where the cowboys and the cattle were.

Robert grinned as they rode away. "Goddamn, you

know how to use that iron. Saw a guy once who was a damn good shot, but you can beat him all hollow.''

''Hope so, that's the way I stay alive sometimes.''

''O'Grady, just how do we convince the cowboys to go along with our plans?''

The federal agent looked at him in surprise in the faint moonlight. ''How? Robert, that was your job, you were supposed to come up with some strategy and some line of discussion that would convince the cowboys to join us.''

''Me? I didn't know. You never told me anything.''

Then Canyon couldn't help but laugh, and soon Robert joined in as they rode toward the cowboys' ranch.

14

The two riders found the cattle herd just before sunup. It was spread in a small valley next to the wagon road, and as the light strengthened, Canyon O'Grady figured there were about two hundred head of mixed cows, calves, steers, and range bulls.

Half a mile across the valley the agent spotted a thin trail of smoke rising straight up from a cabin's chimney. They turned that way.

"If anybody sees us, that tough supervisor is gonna find out and he'll come riding out to meet us," Robert said. "Almost nobody gets to ride a horse except the cowboys. He'll be just curious as hell."

"Good, we'll string him along awhile, see for sure which side he's on."

"Won't be much problem there. He's pure bastard, always looking for a fight, from what I heard."

They were still a quarter of a mile from the cabin when a rider came from behind a second nearby barn and rode toward them at an easy lope.

As the rider came closer, O'Grady realized he was a small man, maybe not much over five feet tall. He rode low in the saddle, slumping a little perhaps to lower his profile even more. He had on a wide-brimmed hat well-curled at the sides and trail-worn. The small man was clean-shaven and his eyes showed the cowboy squint of a man who spends most of his time in the wide open spaces. A revolver rested naturally in a holster at his right side.

"Good morning. Are you the supervisor out here?" Canyon asked, taking the lead and the advantage of an interrogator.

"Yeah, that's right. Utley."

"Good. Colonel Daniel will be coming through this morning sometime with a group of twenty men. They may want to stop here and have your people check their gear and see if they need any replacement horses. The ones they have might not be the best for riding all the way to Fort Collins."

The supervisor's suspicions vanished and he lifted his brows. "Fort Collins?"

"Sure, it's the big invasion. The colonel is going to capture the town with his twenty Royal Guards."

"We have to sit out here all day, or do you have some breakfast cooking in there?" Robert demanded. "The captain here doesn't like to be kept waiting."

The supervisor bobbed his head. "Sure, sure, right this way. Cook is just getting things warmed up."

"Sounds good," Canyon said, and they rode for the ranch house.

They tied up out front, went in, and had a good breakfast. Some of the cowboys came, but they were kept outside until the "captain" and his lieutenant were finished.

Canyon pushed his plate away and stood, then settled the six-gun on his hip.

"Now, I want to have a word with your men before breakfast. Get them all together outside."

"Yes, sir," the supervisor said, and hurried out the door.

"Pushing it?" Robert asked.

"Just getting started," O'Grady said with a grin. He finished his cup of coffee and went out the door, where half a dozen men waited. They looked at him with curiosity. Most of the cowhands looked as they would on any western spread: some tall, some short, all weathered, and about half with full beards to protect their face from the elements, summer or winter.

The supervisor came back with the last half-dozen men. There were twelve riders, enough to handle a herd ten times as big as they had seen. One point was unusual for a cowboy: none of the men wore a gun belt or a weapon of any kind.

The supervisor walked over to O'Grady and nodded. "They're all here. We're getting a trail-drive herd ready. Due to leave in two days. Hope this won't hold us up any."

"It could."

Canyon turned to the cowboys. "Men, this won't take long. I think you're going to like what I have to tell you. As you might know, there's been some trouble in the village and some problems with the Royal Guards. The fact is the King of Colorado is in real trouble."

O'Grady looked at the supervisor, but he got no reaction.

"What I'm telling you is that there is a revolution taking place, and I'm here to enlist your aid."

The supervisor's eyes grew wide. He looked at O'Grady. "My God! How bad is it? Will they come out here?"

"Indeed they will, Utley. In fact, Robert and I are the first elements of the revolution. We're here to hang you for high crimes and to enlist the aid of these cowboys in our revolt to free the citizens of the valley."

Realizing his mistake, the supervisor quivered in anger; his hand jolted for his six-gun but Canyon's draw was faster. His revolver came up and blasted off a .44 round before the supervisor's iron was completely out of his holster.

O'Grady's round had been aimed low and it tore through Utley's right thigh and spun him around. He held on to the weapon as he hit the ground and rolled to his back.

"Drop it, Utley, or you're dead," O'Grady barked.

The supervisor sat up and lifted the six-gun. Canyon's second shot took the man in the right shoulder and slammed the weapon from Utley's hand. It jolted him backward into the dirt.

One of the cowboys cheered. Then the rest of them realized they could cheer too, and a great shout went up. One of the men ran over and kicked Utley in the side.

O'Grady fired again in the air. "Enough," he bellowed. "Just because Utley's an animal is no reason to drop to his level. Somebody get a rope and tie him up. Somebody else bind up his wounds. We want him to live for a court of law to bring to justice. Didn't he hang somebody out here?"

"Damn right he did," one of the cowboys said. "He hung Will Jordan not three months ago. All Will did was try to ride out one afternoon."

"Keep him alive. Now, about the rest of it. We're going to start the revolution. Colonel Daniel will be coming through here this morning with twenty men, all carrying Henry rifles. I broke the firing pins off eighteen of them, so they can't fire. How many of you men want to help me meet the colonel and stop him and start a revolt?"

There were more shouts and cheers and hoorahs, and every man lifted his hand.

"I was figuring maybe we could have that herd down in the valley across the main trail, and when the Colonel comes with his troops, we could stampede those cattle right into the ranks."

"Damn good idea," one man shouted.

"We've got a few hours. You men go in and have a good breakfast. Tell the cook to fix anything you want. This is the first day of the revolt and of your freedom."

The cowboys charged the house and the kitchen. The

cook had heard all of it, and he was grinning as much as the others.

O'Grady talked to several of the cowboys as they waited for breakfast to find out who the leader in the group was. It turned out to be a tall man, Texas-thin, with a wide grin and two missing front teeth. Everyone called him Fang and he didn't mind.

He and Canyon talked for ten minutes, then shook hands.

With breakfast over, the men saddled their mounts and O'Grady saw that most of them were fine cattle horses, sleek and ready for work. They rode to the valley and herded the two hundred head across the main trail and kept them there. They covered nearly a hundred yards across the trail, and most could graze and keep in place.

Fang sent a lookout down the trail almost to the checkpoint to watch for the colonel and his troops.

Then they waited.

Canyon spoke with Fang. "How could Utley keep you men here? You all had horses. He couldn't lock them up every night."

Fang laughed. "No, but he could lock up us men every night, which he did. The man he hung took off in daylight when he was supposed to bring back some cattle that had wandered up a gully. He just kept on going. Utley's a good man on a horse. He lit out after Will, caught him, shot him in the leg, and brought him back. Next day he hung poor Will and made us watch. After that no man was going to ride away unless he was sure he could get away clean. We just didn't have the chance."

"Things will be different now. This kingdom is going to fall today. Tomorrow somebody will be needed to run a ranch here. You've got too many hands, but some of them will want to move on anyway, knowing cowboys."

An hour later the scout came back. He told Fang

that the group of twenty or so horses was coming at a canter and should be along within a half-hour.

"Any more weapons around the place?" O'Grady asked.

They went through Utley's room and found a pair of pistols and a Henry rifle. All were loaded. Canyon gave a pistol to Fang. They armed four of the other cowboys, using Robert's pistol and O'Grady's Henry and the two other arms from the supervisor's digs.

They now had eight armed men in the group of fourteen cowboys. If the Henry firing pins hadn't been replaced, the riders coming at them might have only two weapons that would fire.

All fourteen of the cowboys rode around the front of the herd. On signal they would fire weapons and hoorah the steers and cattle straight to the rear toward the oncoming colonel and his army. They had to start the stampede early enough so the colonel wouldn't run his men around the cattle, but not so early that the running cattle would stretch out and have little effect on the riders.

Canyon waited by the timber side of the cattle. He would force the colonel and his riders back into the herd if they tried to go his way. All the men were in their positions.

Soon the riders came around the small bend in the main trail about a quarter of a mile from the herd. Colonel Daniel came forward, probably expecting the riders to move the animals out of the way for such a grand and important person such as he was.

He held that idea twenty yards too far. Then his men were within forty yards of the steers and range bulls and cows. O'Grady gave the signal with a round fired from his six-gun. Half a dozen other weapons fired and fourteen men charged the animals. The herd panicked.

Soon all two hundred head had turned, bellowing as

they ran full speed away from the strange noises and war whoops near them.

Colonel Daniel was trapped between the onrushing cattle and his surprised troops. He turned and tried to ride to the rear, but he had given no command and the men sat on their mounts, stunned by the mass of animals charging down on them.

The colonel and two men charged to the left into the woods and out of the way of the cattle. But most of the mounted men could not even get their horses into motion before the cattle swarmed around them and over them. One man went down in the melee of flashing horns and pounding feet.

Others held on to their horses' necks and manes as the flood of brown and gray and black bovine backs flashed past them.

Directly behind the cattle came the fourteen cowboys. The seven with weapons had them out and ready.

As the last calf bawled and ran after its mother past the Royal Guards and their civilian fillers, O'Grady rode up and bellowed out orders. "All you men who are not Royal Guards, ride over this way slowly with your hands in the air. Do it now."

Nine men rode slowly to one side. One man on the ground limped after them, grinning as he went.

A shot sounded from the brush and Fang grabbed his shoulder, but he lifted his pistol and fired three times into the brush, then rode out of range of the woods.

Canyon motioned all of his cowboys back out of pistol range of the forest as well, then barked at the civilian guards. "You men, dismount and lead your horses this way. If any man touches his Henry rifle, he's dead. We'll shoot to kill, remember that."

Fang took four of the cowboys and told them to drop their reins and leave their horses. He herded the ten guards with his four cowboys toward the middle of the little valley, where he had them sit down on the grass and wait. He then galloped back toward Canyon.

Back near the trail, O'Grady reloaded the two rounds he had used, tamping the linen prepackaged powder and ball into the cylinder of his army revolver. He checked the second cylinder in his jacket pocket.

He had altered the percussion revolver so the whole cylinder would come out by releasing a small lever. Then a new cylinder, already loaded with five or six rounds, could be snapped into place and he would have a new batch of rounds to fire much quicker than if he had to load the cylinders one at a time.

"I'm going in to get the colonel," O'Grady said.

Fang looked up. "I've done some shooting. I'll come with you."

The agent shook his head. "Not your job, Fang. You hold the prisoners, talk to the civilians, and see if they want to help us man the revolt. We'll get started for town as soon as I can find the colonel."

He turned and rode into the woods well below where he had seen the colonel enter it.

15

Rapidly Canyon O'Grady catalogued what he knew about the situation at the kingdom's ranch. The colonel had taken two men with him into the woods, and both must have had Henry repeating rifles. But neither of those men had fired at the cowboys.

Therefore, the rifles must not be able to fire. That left the trio with one six-gun. He assumed that Colonel Daniel would be able to reload the percussion revolver in the woods. All three men were mounted. O'Grady rode into the woods fifty yards and stopped and listened. Nothing. He was about to move when a revolver shot slammed through the stillness, the round skimming over his head by inches.

Canyon jerked the big palomino to the side and surged behind a pair of tall firs. He watched for the blue smoke and saw where it rose ghostlike around the side of a piñon. The gunman was probably mounted. The smoke started too high for a man on the ground.

O'Grady pulled his own Henry from the boot and levered a shell into it, then he sent a round nipping the bark from the side of the piñon where the man had fired from.

There was no reaction. It must have been the colonel who fired. He wouldn't trust the loaded weapon to anyone else. Cautiously, Canyon slid off the palomino. He could see that the animal's hind quarters showed past the pair of trees. He doubted the colonel would waste a shot on a horse's ass.

Now O'Grady started earning his money. He worked through some low brush and small trees that concealed him as he moved at right angles to the tree that had been used. He had heard no sounds from a horse, no movement, so the man and rider must still be there.

Canyon used all of his skill in moving through the brush without making it shake or shiver. He bent double and crept along carefully, not breaking a twig or letting a branch snap back. Just past a medium-sized ponderosa pine, he checked toward the spot where he had seen the smoke puff.

Now he had a better angle on the area and could see halfway behind the tree. Colonel Daniel lay beside the tree, staring through the leaves in the direction where O'Grady had been. One of his legs moved outward to give him a firmer firing position on the ground. His horse stood tied to one side.

Canyon grinned. He lifted the Henry, aimed down the sights at the colonel's thigh, and squeezed off the round. The heavy .44-caliber slug dug into flesh, jolted off the big bone, and exploded out the other side of his thigh, taking a handful of flesh with it.

The colonel screamed in frustrated and anguished torment. When he could find his speaking voice again, he bellowed out his rage. "You'll have to kill me, redhead. I won't ever let you capture me. Come and get me!" He fired once at the tree where the smoky black powder had given away Canyon's position.

"Use up your rounds, Colonel. Then it will be easy."

"I've got more than a hundred. I'll still be here by nightfall."

Canyon could see the toe of the colonel's boot. The secret agent lifted the rifle and fired, but the bullet missed the boot. It was quickly withdrawn.

There came the merest hint of a sound, but Canyon heard it and brought up his pistol as he whirled around where he lay behind the tree. One of the men with the colonel had slipped in back of O'Grady's position and under cover of the talk had moved up within striking distance.

The noise was enough to alert O'Grady, who saw the body flying through the air at him, a gleaming knife already on its downward plunge.

The .44 round O'Grady fired hit the diving man in the throat, carried away part of his windpipe and half of his jugular vein, and the attacker fell short of his target. He rolled over and the knife dropped from his fingers. He looked at Canyon, then shook his head as he died.

When O'Grady glanced back at the tree where Colonel Daniel had hidden, he knew the man was gone. There was no physical evidence, it was just not the same.

Twenty yards away Canyon heard a saddle creak and he leapt up and raced for Cormac. He mounted the big stallion and galloped out of the woods and down the road fifty yards on the trail, then he edged back into the woods to wait and watch. The colonel would go this way, Canyon thought. He must have money or jewels back at the village and figured he could get them and get away into the hills before the real revolution got that far.

O'Grady sat there five minutes, listening with every pore and every nerve ending in his entire body. He was just about to move on for a new bite of the trail when he heard some noise behind him: the soft murmur of a horse's voice. The colonel had ridden through the brush and trees much slower than Canyon thought he would.

O'Grady dropped off his mount, ground-tied him, and slipped another twenty feet into the forest, angling for a sizable blue spruce. He got to it just as he saw the sorrel coming through some leaves to his right.

The agent waited, and when he figured the colonel should be about fifteen feet away by the sound of the horse, Canyon stepped out, a six-gun in each hand, both aimed at the surprised chief of security for the Kingdom of Colorado.

Colonel Daniel dived off the far side of his horse and both O'Grady's revolvers fired. One round took the colonel in the shoulder as he vanished. The horse spurted forward and Canyon went in after the fallen colonel.

Before the agent could fire or even get out a word, another horse thundered down almost on top of him. The big Irishman had time only to dive to his left to avoid the flying hooves of a big roan ridden by a man who was headed directly at him. Even as he dived away from the animal, he felt his left leg pang with pain as one of the horse's back hooves kicked him as it galloped by.

O'Grady lifted up in surprise and anger. He had the bastard and then he was gone. Where did he go? He looked at the spot where the colonel had fallen but all he found were some splotches of blood. Unless the colonel was an exceptional horseman he could not have been picked up by the rider on the charging roan horse. That had been the second man who got away with the colonel, Canyon thought.

He found lots of sign that the colonel had indeed left the area on foot. He was limping, his steps uneven. Here and there was a drop of fresh blood. Weeds and grass showed plainly where they had been bent forward as boots had crushed them.

Canyon followed the trail for thirty or forty feet at a time, then looked ahead to be sure he wasn't walking into an ambush. Soon it cut for the open land along the valley. As soon as he had the general direction, O'Grady ran ahead with the Henry held in both hands in front of him.

He burst out of the brush to the wagon road and looked north toward the village. They were not yet at the checkpoint. A small bend in the road ahead concealed the way before him. O'Grady ran about fifty yards to the bend in the road, and there, less than a hundred yards ahead, he saw the roan and two men starting to mount up.

Canyon went to his stomach and raised the rifle's butt plate up to his shoulder. His first round centered on the horse. He hated killing an animal, but this time it was a necessity.

He fired. The head shot put the horse down in a screaming death cry. Canyon tracked the other men in the rifle sights. He was not sure which one was which now. He picked one and fired. The man screamed, then fell to the ground and didn't move.

The second man had bolted for the woods. Now O'Grady saw that the man was limping heavily, and he knew it had to be the colonel. The U.S. agent fired twice. The first shot missed and the second splintered against a willow tree the colonel had thrown himself behind.

O'Grady lifted off the ground and ran forward. He had lost count how many rounds he had left in the Henry. He charged along the open land toward the dead horse, then turned into the woods, moving from cover to cover, allowing no easy shot for the colonel, who still had the revolver.

Canyon stopped dead-still and listened. He heard soft footsteps to his left, north again, then a wild spurt of a dozen steps before they stopped again.

The big Irishman bolted in the direction of the sound, jolting from one pine tree to the next, scanning the area ahead of him for any sign of life.

He stopped behind a fir and listened. More light steps. Canyon charged forward again, closing the range rapidly.

The round came before he expected it and when he was between his two points of cover. A bullet nicked him in the arm. Blood, but no real damage. He got to his cover tree, squatted down, and peered around from ground level.

He saw the colonel lying behind a fallen log and panting, his six-gun resting on top of it.

O'Grady sighted in with the Henry and fired. The colonel's percussion revolver flew off the tree trunk as if someone had tugged it with a string.

A wailing moan came from behind the log.

"Give it up, Colonel. Your war is over. You lost. We have your troops, we have your guns, soon we'll have your king. Give it up and live."

"Shit, yes. Live for how long? Those bastard cowboys will roast me alive. You think I made friends here? Who the hell are you anyway, redhead?"

"I'm a federal agent sent in to find out what happened to the U.S. mail you stole along with those stagecoaches. Hell, nobody minded a few stages, but when you fuck around with the United States post office, you're asking for a whole lot of hell to be poured down your open fly."

"You don't talk like a government man."

"That's why they keep me around. So stand up. Both your men are gone. You've got at least two bullets in you. Stand up and surrender."

"Not a chance in hell, government man."

The pistol shot came as a surprise and O'Grady ducked back behind the big tree.

"Isn't that a little underpowered going up against a Henry repeater, Colonel?" Canyon shouted.

"A man uses what he has. I'll probably be using my knife next, and last my fists," Daniel yelled.

"It doesn't have to end that way."

"The hell it doesn't. I played my last card in a game I thought I could win. I lost. You could at least do the right thing for me."

"What's that, Colonel?"

"I'll stand up and you blow my brains out with that Henry."

"I can't do that, Colonel."

"Figured you wouldn't. At least you're calling me colonel."

"What was your real rank in the army before you went over the hill?"

"Made corporal after three years, then I got tired of taking orders."

Before O'Grady could get ready, the colonel lunged as best he could over the log and charged him. His little hideout .32 derringer held in front of him with one more shot in the chamber.

"Now I've got you, you dirty bastard," Colonel Daniel screeched madly as he charged forward, his shot-up leg forgotten, his face a mask of anger and hate, and one bloody arm hanging useless at his side.

Later, Canyon would have no conscious memory of aiming. His six-gun came up from his side and he fired three times, all three slugs jolting into Colonel Daniel's chest. The last one stopped his forward motion and he dropped to his knees and then collapsed on his chest, his face smacking the mulch below the ancient fir trees.

O'Grady ran to him, but he was already dead. The agent lifted the corpse by one arm and one leg, hoisting him onto his shoulders. He grabbed the Henry and then walked down to the edge of the woods and lay the man on the wagon trail.

Canyon whistled and a moment later his palomino pranced out of the edge of the brush and trotted up to him. The Irishman swung on board and galloped back to the ranch.

When he got there, the cattle was grazing in the valley again and a row of horses were tethered at the rails in front of the ranch house. He pulled up and tied Cormac.

Fang came out. "Get him?"

"I did. You men ready to start a revolution?"

"We already did. We had a meeting. Since you

weren't here, you didn't get to vote. Utley killed a friend of ours, so we decided to return the favor.'' Fang pointed to a gnarled oak tree near the barn. From one sturdy limb hung a small body swinging slowly in the wind.

"It's done," Canyon said, grimacing. "Get everyone together. I'll talk to the men as we ride. Now the main part of our work begins."

16

"What about them damn Royal Guards?" Fang asked Canyon O'Grady as the men poured from the ranch house.

"From what I've heard, most of them did what they were told," O'Grady said. "Some of them were drafted into the job."

Fang drew a line in the dust with his boot. "Hell, the ones I talked to didn't seem like such bad *hombres*. Reckon we could turn them loose?"

Canyon had been wondering about the same thing. "Get them together, I'll talk to them."

Five minutes later O'Grady had told them what was about to happen. He invited any of them who cared to, to join in the uprising. Those who didn't want to, could turn east and walk out to the Denver road.

Two of them stared hard at O'Grady.

"You're not wanting us to get off a bit so you could have some target practice, now, are you?" one rangy man with a slight southern accent asked.

"No," O'Grady barked. "If I say you can go free, you can go. No doubts. No one here will lift a weapon. Just move if you want to, and do it now."

The two turned and headed for the trail out to the main road to Denver. Fang send a rider to tail the men out for a couple of miles, then told him to catch up with them on the way to town.

O'Grady had the rest of the former Royal Guards

take off their red caps and jackets. Most of them did so with a whoop of joy.

By the time they were all mounted and ready to move, Canyon had a force of eight former guards, twelve cowboys, himself, and Robert.

They took along three spare horses and figured on recruiting some farmers to ride them.

"First we have the checkpoint to take over," O'Grady said. He put the eight men with guns in the front ranks, and they soon rounded a bend so they could see the checkpoint. The bar was still across the wagon road.

When they were a hundred yards away, Canyon lifted the troop to a trot and then a gallop and charged down on the checkpoint.

"One round each into the checkpoint," O'Grady yelled. The eight men in front fired, and before they pulled up, the two guards came out with their hands held high over their heads.

The man Canyon had shot earlier now had a white bandage on his leg. He stared at the collection of riders and shook his head. "Who are you guys?"

"We're a mounted posse from Denver come to clean out this rat's nest of outlaws," Canyon brayed. "We're hanging anyone who opposes us. You want to hang, or you want to come ride with us?"

"Hell, we're just following orders," the man said, not recognizing O'Grady. "We've got two horses. We can join you."

"You have any firearms here that work?" Canyon asked. The other went into the shack and brought out three revolvers, fully loaded, and one Henry rifle and a muzzle-loading flintlock.

Ten minutes later the twenty-five horsemen rode steadily toward town. It was just after nine o'clock in the morning.

When they came to the first settlements, O'Grady sent two horsemen to each of the farms with specific instructions to have all the men and women arm themselves with pitchforks, axes, knives, and hatchets and join the group of riders.

The rest of the horsemen dismounted and waited. Twenty minutes later they saw the first cluster of farmers coming.

The walkers waved to Canyon's man and grinned and laughed.

"It really true?" a blonde asked, running toward them. "We really going to march on the castle and overthrow the king?"

"We most certainly are, ma'am," Canyon said. "Just as soon as we get there with as many people as we can bring along."

The swelling group began to move forward and the distances between farms grew shorter. By noon they were almost at the outskirts of the village. Now volunteers from the farms ran from house to house spreading the word and mustering up new support.

O'Grady sent riders through the streets yelling out the news, urging the people out of their houses and shops.

"We're rousting out the king today," the horsemen called. "Everyone out to march on the king. We're going to be free!"

Their progress slowed as they worked through the streets of houses and businesses. Some people refused to come, saying they supported the idea, but they were not going to march.

Canyon sent Robert riding toward the palace to see what was going on there. When he got within a block of the big log building he saw a line of twenty red-capped supervisors standing in the square. The men were armed with their batons and twirled them nervously.

Robert rode back and reported what he had seen.

Canyon gathered his thirteen riders with weapons and told them about the line of supervisors. "The thirteen of us will be in the front rank. I'll give them an ultimatum, and if they don't give up, we'll fire one shot each at the men and then charge the line with our mounts. Everyone understand? No one fires until I give the order.''

The crowd behind the horses was well over a hundred by now. They were still two blocks from the castle.

O'Grady took his twenty-four horsemen and marched them forward twelve abreast across the wide street. When they came around the corner to the square, the supervisors were still in line, blocking the way to the castle.

O'Grady pulled his riders to a halt in a ragged line about twenty yards from the supervisors. ''Men, the Kingdom of Colorado is smashed, the king is dethroned. Democracy is returning to this land. If you want to stand there and defy us, a lot of you are going to get killed. If not, all you have to do is take off those red hats, throw them in the dirt, drop your clubs, and walk forward past our mounts and join the popular uprising.''

None of the men moved. One near the center wavered, but he held fast.

Halfway down the line of O'Grady's group of armed men, one of them fired his Henry rifle and a supervisor toppled to the ground, dead. Everyone froze.

''Damned guy raped my daughter,'' the shooter shouted in his own defense.

Canyon ignored the incident. ''You men have one more chance,'' he bellowed. ''There might be reprisals for any of your past illegal actions, but in a court of law with a jury. Who wants to save his skin? Move now.''

Three of the guards dropped their batons and walked forward, stripping off their hats, and squeezing past the thin line of horses to the rear.

Sixteen men remained.

Canyon felt the people moving close to him behind the line of horses. "Men, ready your pieces and take aim," he barked.

As O'Grady shouted the order, two more men broke from the ranks of supervisors and rushed forward, tossing away their caps.

"Retreat," one of the supervisors bellowed. The fourteen men left ran from the crowd.

"Fire," Canyon boomed, and the thirteen weapons went off, then the pistols fired again.

Six of the supervisors stumbled and fell. The men on horseback tore forward, riding to the steps of the palace and clamoring there on their mounts.

By now almost every man and woman in the village hurried up to the castle or stood there watching. Most of them had some kind of weapon.

Someone started a chant. "Down with the king! Down with the king!" Soon the whole three hundred people chanted the words.

A shadowy figure appeared in one of the second-story windows and stepped outside and fired a pistol at the crowd, but the gunman was too far away and the round fell short.

One of the riflemen lifted his weapon, but O'Grady shouted for him to lower it.

A moment later the big doors of the castle opened and a Royal Guards lieutenant stepped out. He held a pistol in one hand and behind him ten Royal Guards in uniform hurried out to flank him. They all carried Henry rifles with bayonets attached.

The lieutenant held up both hands for silence, but boos and screams of rage came from the crowd.

O'Grady lifted up in his stirrups and fired a shot in the air. The sound caused the people to hush and he charged up to the lieutenant.

"Let this man have his say," O'Grady bellowed to the crowd behind him. He turned back to the lieutenant.

The young man held up his left hand again. His right he kept near his pistol.

"The King of Colorado—"

There was an instant booing.

"We ain't got no king," a voice shouted.

"Down with the damn king," another said.

"The king says that if all of you go back to your homes and shops in a peaceful manner, he will not penalize anyone for this outrage. The king says that a two-day holiday will be held, starting now, to celebrate our good harvest and our two years of the Kingdom of Colorado."

Again the crowd booed and yelled and screamed.

A pistol shot rang out and one of the Royal Guards behind the lieutenant took a slug in the shoulder. He backed out of the line and fell to his knees, holding his wound as blood seeped through his fingers.

"Is that all you have to tell these good people who the king has kept in slavery for two years?" O'Grady shouted.

The lieutenant backed up a step. He watched the crowd and Canyon. The man gave a quiet order and the nine Royal Guards lifted their Henry rifles, with three of them aimed at Canyon O'Grady.

"Prepare to fire," the lieutenant said. "Ready, aim—"

Before he could give the order to fire, Canyon drew his own six-gun and put a bullet squarely into the lieutenant's chest. He fell backward. Now the rest of Canyon's rebellious gunmen fired and four of the Royal Guards collapsed to the wooden porch. Those able to move rushed into the castle and slammed the door shut.

O'Grady motioned to Robert and both men dropped off their horses and ran to the first-floor windows. Pistol butts smashed through the two-foot-square windows, and both men squirmed through and into the quarters of the guards. No one was there. Robert cocked his pistol and rushed for the door. A guard came running into the room and took a slug in the head from Robert's weapon and careened to the wall, then slid to the floor.

In the hall there was confusion as guards rushed around not knowing what to do. One tried to fire his Henry at O'Grady, but the broken firing pin left the rifle useless.

"Get to the main door and throw it open for the people," Canyon said to Robert.

O'Grady hurried for the stairs to the second floor. One guard stood there with his useless rifle. He dropped the weapon and lifted his hands.

"Where is the princess's room?" Canyon demanded. The man pointed left. "Take me there," the U.S. agent snapped.

The guard turned and hurried down the hall to the fourth door and pointed.

Canyon didn't bother to knock; he simply pushed open the door and rushed inside.

Melissa had been watching the crowd from behind a curtained window. She wore a long red gown. There were tears in her eyes. She saw O'Grady and ran to him, her arms held wide.

He held her a moment then kissed her cheek. "Get into some more ordinary clothes; we have to disguise you for a few hours until the anger of the crowd dies down. Hurry!"

She looked at him, then stammered out the words. "I—I can't while you're here."

"Now is no time for modesty. That crowd might tear you apart." He ripped the bodice of the gown open and lifted the skirt and pulled it off over her head. Three of the four petticoats followed. She had on only a chemise and drawers that extended from waist down her legs to the knees.

"The blue skirt you wear when you're picking flowers," O'Grady said. "Hurry, we don't have much time."

She slid into the skirt and then drew on a faded blue shirt like most of the people wore.

Canyon looked at the balcony. He motioned her that way. "The trellis, have you ever climbed down it?"

She nodded.

"Good! I don't think it would hold me. You start down, then I'll jump. Quickly!"

As soon as Melissa had worked halfway to the ground, Canyon slipped over the edge, climbed down the rough logs until he was four feet from the ground, then jumped. He landed on his feet and then caught Melissa as she fell the last three feet. He took her hand and they hurried toward the woods. So far none of the citizens had come around to the back of the castle.

"What are they going to do?" Melissa asked, wide-eyed.

"I don't know. Whatever it is, I don't want you to see it. None of this was your doing. So you must stay here out of sight until I come for you, even if it isn't until after dark. Promise?"

She leaned against him. Her arms went around him and she shivered. He held her tightly until the shivering stopped. She tried to talk, but couldn't, and then nodded, tears brimming in her eyes.

"I'll be back as quickly as I can. You stay here hidden. If anyone finds you, say you are in from one of the farms and got lost."

O'Grady rushed away from her, paused at the edge of the woods, but saw no one at the back of the castle or looking out the windows. He ran around the far end of the castle wall and toward the front, hoping he could get there before the citizens, who had turned into an angry mob, did anything that couldn't be undone, come morning.

17

Canyon ran around the front corner of the palace and saw dozens of people charging in and out of the big structure. He was relieved to see there was some semblance of order. The dead men who fell at the front of the palace had been carried away in a wagon and put in the undertaker's building.

A tall man with gray hair and spectacles had put down the ax he carried, and now was calmly directing search parties. He seemed to carry an air of authority.

Fang came up to the man and spoke a few moments, then he hurried off. The cowboy still carried the pistol he had used earlier in the day. He came toward O'Grady.

"There you are! We've been looking for you. We can't find Klingman. That's who used to be king. His name is Jacob Klingman, ya know, and he also used to be the preacher here in the commune. Elder Teincuff wants to talk to you."

"He the old one you were just speaking to?"

"Right. He used to be the head elder of the commune, did most of the day-to-day operations. He's a smart man, and a devoted Christian as well. Everyone here looks up to him."

"When you find the ex-king, try to take him alive," O'Grady said. "The people will want to see justice done the democratic way."

Fang grinned. "Just about what the elder told me.

We've got it narrowed down now. I better get with my men.''

O'Grady walked up to the man Fang had called Elder Teincuff, who was speaking softly to a man with fire in his eyes. The man nodded at last and ran back toward the big log structure.

"Elder Teincuff?" Canyon said as he walked toward him.

"Yes." The man's green eyes led his smile. "You must be that redhead I've heard about, Canyon O'Grady." He held out his hand and they shook warmly. "It's a great service you've done us here this day, Mr. O'Grady. We'll forever appreciate it. We know things can't go back to the way they were in the commune, but we'll form a good village here, establish things the democratic way, and be ready to take our place in the Colorado Territory when it qualifies.''

"It's part of my job, Elder Teincuff. I work for the federal government.''

"I wondered about that.''

"Elder Teincuff, I hope we can control the people so the girl won't be harmed. She had no part in this. She hated what her father was doing.''

"I agree, and I've already given such instructions to the people. We're really not an overly violent group, but tempers have been rather high today.''

"I would guess that anyone who wishes to leave the area now will be free to go, except those guards and supervisors you may wish to prosecute," Canyon said.

"We citizens have arrested six guards so far and four supervisors who have serious felony criminal charges that will be brought. But first we must deal with the ex-king, Jacob Klingman. I'm afraid leniency will not be coming for him.''

"We found the bastard," a voice boomed out from the third floor of the castle. The people below cheered. More people gathered around the castle doors, but they were surprisingly silent and watchful. When the ex-king was brought from the big double doors, he already had a rope around his neck with a hangman's knot in it.

Elder Teincuff frowned and hurried to the steps and ordered the rope removed. He looked around and decided the steps would be the best place for Jacob Klingman to stand.

"Teincuff, it's come to this?" Klingman said, watching the man. "You turn on me too, just when we're about to expand the kingdom. How could you do that, Teincuff? Didn't I give you the best job in the kingdom?"

Elder Teincuff shook his head and watched the ex-king. "Jacob, you gave us only fear and worry and death. You were a better pastor than a king. Now be quiet." Teincuff held up both hands and the crowd of over three hundred quieted almost at once.

"Ladies and gentlemen, I have no official rank here, but some urged me to help us through this euphoric and cataclysmic few hours. I'll be your acting mayor for now. Tomorrow we will hold open filing for nomination petitions for a more permanent mayor and six city councilmen who will later be elected by a vote of each man and woman over the age of eighteen years.

"That's tomorrow. This afternoon we need to decide what to do with our ex-leader, Jacob Klingman. As all of you know, this man is charged with more than a dozen murders, complicity in another dozen deaths, the unlawful seduction and rape of more than thirty of our women. As of now, this court of the people so charges him.

"All of those present who wish to vote guilty to these charges against Jacob Klingman, say aye."

There was a thunderous response.

"All those present who wish to vote innocent to these charges against Jacob Klingman, vote nay."

Not a single voice could be heard.

"Bastards," Klingman roared. "You aren't men,

you're sheep. You don't know a good government when you have one. How many of you went hungry? How many of you were cold in the winter? How many of you were without gainful employment?'' He shook his head in anger and frustration.

Elder Teincuff watched Klingman for a moment. When the ex-king stopped, he went on. "Therefore, by the temporary power vested in me by this assembly, I find the defendant guilty as charged. The only penalty can be death. How am I advised that it should be carried out?''

A man in the front row stepped forward and held up his hand.

"Yes, Johnson," Teincuff said.

"I say we hang him. Hanging will give him more time to worry about it and to realize he done wrong.''

"Dammit! I've done nothing wrong," Klingman roared. "Why can't you accept that?''

Another man rose and was recognized. "Most of the people he killed or had killed died from gunshots. I think we should execute him by a firing squad, but not until dawn. That'd give him a few hours to think about what he's done.''

"Bastards! Ungrateful bastards," Klingman brayed. "I brought you all here. I carved this community out of the wilderness. How can you turn on me this way?''

A third man lifted his hand. "Teincuff, I guess it's time we did this right to this crazy man. I think we should get us four plow horses and attach one to each of his arms and legs and whip them horses in four different directions and tear that son—tear him to pieces.''

A small cheer went up.

There was a quiet spell when no one spoke.

Elder Teincuff watched the people. "If I may offer a suggestion . . . The Bible teaches us an eye for an eye. We certainly can't execute Jacob Klingman thirty times. But the suffering idea is a valid one. Many of the people he had killed fell under the cat-o'-nine-tails.

"It would be my suggestion that every man who was whipped by the king's men be allowed to give one lash across the convicted killer's body. That might be thirty-five or forty, and would be more than any man could live through."

"I so move," a man in the front row said.

Elder Teincuff nodded. "In favor, signify by saying aye."

There was a thunderous vote of ayes.

"Opposed signify by saying nay."

Half a dozen voices rang out.

"Motion is carried. The post will be readied at once. The whips will be found. The execution will take place as soon as the arrangements can be made."

Klingman screamed again and started to run down the steps. Two men grabbed him and pushed him down to his knees on the steps. They stood near him so he couldn't run again.

Teincuff signaled to some men to begin getting the whipping post ready.

"Now for a related matter. Many of us have known and loved a young girl for five years, some of us for three years before that. It is my suggestion that Melissa Jacob not be tainted with the sins of her father, that she be given the freedom to stay with us or to go, and that her safety becomes the vital concern of every man and woman in this community as long as she is among us. Does this meet with this assembly's approval?"

A roll of ayes filled the air and Teincuff smiled.

The men to use the whip began lining up to one side. Elder Teincuff left the steps and talked to each one. Some he simply nodded at. One or two he asked to see their backs. One man he eliminated from the line.

The post was positioned in the grassy square and readied.

O'Grady watched with interest. This was basic republic-type government, where every voter cast his ballot on each item of governmental work. He was fascinated by how many men had lined up for the punishment. He counted and came to forty-four.

The sun brimmed the far peaks of the Rocky Mountains to the west as the condemned man was brought to the pole. He was stripped to the waist and his hands thrust through the iron rings and tied behind the foot-thick log.

Then Elder Teincuff held up his hands and the people quieted. "Does the condemned man have any last words?"

Jacob Klingman turned and stared at his former deputy and shook his head. "I did it all for the good of the commune, Teincuff. We were much more efficient the last two years. My influence was growing. No matter what you say, I am still the King of Colorado. If you must kill the king, then you must."

Teincuff lifted his hand and brought it down pointing at the first man in line. He carried his whip to the spot where he had seen the whip man stand, judged the distance, and swung the leathers down hard across the white flesh of Jacob Klingman.

The ex-king bellowed in pain and rage.

The second man took the whip and lashed down with all his might. A second pattern of red welts raised on the tender skin. Again Klingman screamed in pain.

Five men delivered their lashes to the condemned man. The last time he bleated from the pain. Now crossing lines had ruptured and blood ran slowly down the white-and-red flesh.

Six, seven, eight, nine, ten . . . The lashes came with the same angry justice as each man grunted when he lashed the man who had made him suffer for no reason.

On the tenth lash Klingman's head sagged against the post. He whimpered now as each new swing of the lash hit him.

The whip was changed for a new one, since this one was soaked with blood.

Eleven, twelve, thirteen, fourteen, fifteen . . .

Klingman could not lift his head now.

Blood ran in a stream down his back, soaking his pants.

After the twentieth stroke of the whip, people began murmuring in the gathering. One woman called for them to stop.

Elder Teincuff approached the ex-king and touched a finger to his throat artery. A faint pulse still beat.

He stepped back and signaled for the next man to bring the whip.

After thirty lashes he checked again.

The King of Colorado was dead.

People began to drift silently away. It was obvious to everyone that Jacob Klingman was dead, but the rest of the injured men in line could not be denied their one lash.

O'Grady faded back into the crowd and noticed the beginnings of dusk. He had no desire to see the final strokes. Five of the original men at the end of the line shook their heads and gave up their turn.

The last ten men knew that they were whipping a corpse, but it didn't matter. One man muttered that the bastard had nearly killed him with the lash, and he was going to set the scales as even as they would go.

Canyon stepped around the side of the palace and headed for the brush where he had left Melissa. As he walked toward the spot, he saw the young woman step out of the trees and look around.

"No," he said softly, and she heard and then saw him. He ran to her and they went back in the trees and found a spot to sit in the grass.

"I heard some of it," she said, her voice shaking

and her face stained with tears. "They—the people executed my father, didn't they?"

"No, Melissa. That man out there was not your father. Your real father died a dozen years ago in Texas when those Comanche overran his position and killed so many of his men. His spirit died that day, and what was left was a poor shell of a man. He tried everyway he could, but he had been crushed, defeated by a group of people he considered innately inferior to himself.

"I've seen it happen to army officers before. All guts and glory one minute, and then broken, impotent, useless the next. You can't blame yourself. This man you've lived with for the last half of your life wasn't your real father. Haven't you sensed that?"

She nodded, eyes wide. Slowly she leaned against him and cried. "I know, he wasn't my real father, but still I want to cry for him. I want somebody to mourn him, and I'm the only one who will."

He held her tenderly as she cried. It was more than five minutes later that she dried her eyes.

"We won't be staying in the cas—the big log cabin, will we? I want to go down by the stream somewhere. I want to hear it chattering as I go to sleep tonight."

O'Grady said that would be fine. First he had to get his horse. "We'll both be right back. You wait a minute more." He ran to the edge of the palace. The street in front was almost empty of people. The undertaker had lifted the ex-king off his post and put him in a wagon that he hitched a horse to and drove toward his mortuary.

Canyon whistled. Nothing happened. He whistled again and from around a house on a street a block down, the big golden stallion came trotting. He threw his head and cantered along like a king himself down the block and up to the big Irishman.

O'Grady swung atop and rode past the palace to the edge of the woods. He stepped down and lifted Melissa to the steed's broad rear quarters behind the saddle.

"I've ridden before," she said.

He stepped into the saddle. "Let's get away upstream somewhere. It's still light enough so we can see to find a nice camping spot. Then I'll build a small fire and you can tell me what you'll be doing now that you're free to go wherever you want to."

"You mean I'm free to leave?"

"Yes, you're not at fault. Elder Teincuff agreed."

She hugged him tighter and reached up and kissed his cheek.

18

Melissa picked a spot half a mile above the village where the stream narrowed and chattered down a two-foot falls. She sat and threw stones in the water as Canyon used his heavy knife and cut a dozen fir boughs and then trimmed the small branches off them until he had enough for a makeshift mattress.

She came and stood beside him. "I think you're right about Father. He never was the same after we left Texas; something had changed. He never played with me anymore. I was young then and I missed that. Mother told me he'd been sick.

"He was in a hospital for a long time, but sometimes we didn't see him for months at a time anyway. But now that I think how he acted, I know that he just wasn't the same man after he had that big fight with the Comanche."

She watched him build a small fire as darkness closed around them. She shivered. He put his arm around her and drew her close to him.

"There's nothing to be afraid of. No angry animals out there in the dark, no Indians, no supervisors or anyone else who wants to do us any harm. We're safe, so try to relax."

She gave a big sigh, pushed a stick into the fire from where they sat close to it. "Tell me about yourself, Canyon O'Grady. I know nothing about you."

"I came to this country with my parents from Ireland when I was very young—just born, in fact. My father was one of the workers for Irish independence and the British police were hunting for him when we left.

"He went back twice and took me along as a sort of camouflage. While I was there, a band of Catholic monks pounded into me thick Irish skull what little book-learning I've managed. In this country, a lot of Irishmen worked building the railroads, but I didn't fancy that, so I worked my way to Washington, D.C., and became a United States government agent. And, pretty lass, that's about all there is to tell."

"At least it's a little." She turned to face him in the firelight. "Did I tell you I love that wild Irish red hair of yours? It looks like your head is on fire."

"And I like that firm little chin of yours. It's going to get you in trouble sometimes, but you've got the good sense to be practical about it." He bent and kissed her lips tenderly.

"Oh, dear," Melissa breathed when their lips parted. She looked at him and he saw a startled fawn, finding something new and strange and a little scary, but so interesting it couldn't run away.

"Would you—would you please do that again?" she asked, her voice barely a whisper.

He bent and kissed her lips again, and this time her arms went around his neck and held him tightly. She pushed closer to him so her breasts touched his chest, and when she released him, she cuddled against his shoulder.

Melissa sighed and turned a glorious, wistful smile to him. "Why can't it always be this way? Why can't the two of us just stay right here forever and kiss each other and hold each other. I don't think I've ever been happier, more contented, more at peace with the world."

He kissed her nose. "We would get hungry after a while, I'm afraid," he said gently.

She laughed, then got serious. "I want to forget all

of that for as long as I can. There's something much more important I want you to do for me. Right now, I want you to teach me how to make love.''

''You never have?''

''Of course not. I'm not married. I know it starts out with kisses.''

She kissed him again, more serious this time and he touched her lips with his tongue and they parted and he probed gently. Her tongue darted into his mouth and she sighed and they eased over on the softness of the fir tips. She lay partly on top of him.

''That is so strange, so wild.'' She kissed him again, this time with her mouth open, and their tongues battled for a moment, then she let him probe deeply in her mouth and she pushed her breasts hard against him.

His hand came up and found one breast and rubbed it gently through the fabric of the blue shirt.

She pushed him away and sat up. ''I want you to see me, to look at me and tell me if I'm big enough, if I'm like other women.''

She unbuttoned her shirt and pulled it off, then she lifted away the white silk chemise. Melissa sat there in the soft firelight, her shoulders back, her breasts forward.

''Perfect,'' he said. Her breasts were full, set high, with wide bands of pink areolae and pinker yet nipples now starting to rise and grow firm. ''Perfect, just beautiful.'' He caressed them gently, then tweaked her nipples, and she looked up at him quickly.

''Feels wonderful,'' she moaned, her eyes half-closed. ''I'm feeling all soft and warm. I want you to show me more.''

He bent and kissed one breast, and her eyes came open wide. She gasped, then sucked in a big breath and pulled him down on top of her as she shivered.

''What's happening?'' she wailed.

''It's natural, you're having a climax. Just enjoy it.''

He kissed her breasts again and again, and her whole

body shook with one series of spasms after another. She moaned and writhed under him. Slowly the climax tapered off and Melissa opened her eyes. She smiled up at him.

"Oh, glory! So that was a climax. It was . . . I just can't describe it."

"That's just the start of the wonderful feelings, Melissa."

"You'll go—you'll enter me, down below?"

"Yes, if you want me to. That's usually the most wonderful feeling of all." He took her hand and moved it down to the bulge in his pants.

"Oh! Oh, my!"

He unbuttoned his fly and pushed her hand inside. She touched his erection.

"Do you want to look?"

She nodded, sucked in a breath, then nodded again. He took off his boots and pulled down his pants and short underwear, and as he uncovered his crotch, she gasped.

"So big! That will never . . ." She looked up at him. "Canyon, you've done this before and you must know. Will it?"

"Yes, we'll fit together just fine. But not until you're ready and you want me to."

She relaxed a minute. He caressed her breasts again, kissed them, and then kissed down across her chest and her flat little belly toward the top of her skirt.

Melissa caught his face. "Canyon, if I want this, I have to help." She moved him away, then slipped out of her blue skirt and her shoes and stockings. She wore only the pantslike drawers made of soft cotton with a dozen small blue bows of ribbon on them.

She kissed him then, desperately, hugging him tightly, not able to look him in the eye.

"Maybe we should stop for now," he said softly. "We could try again tomorrow."

"No!" Her voice came sharply. "No, I'm being as

prissy as an old maid.'' She unbuttoned the fasteners at both sides of the white drawers, stripped them down, and threw them beside her skirt.

"Please, dearest Canyon O'Grady. Right now, show me how to make love."

Softly, gently he introduced her to the art of making love. She cried out in a brief moment of pain when he first entered her, but then she relaxed and was swept away in thrill and ecstasy.

Twice he showed her the joy of lovemaking, then he let the fire die down, pulled their clothes back on, and they lay close together on the fir boughs.

"I've never been so happy in my life," she said softly. "Now I understand a lot of things I didn't know before. Now I can decide what I want to do with the rest of my life."

She snuggled close to him and his arm went around her. He lay his six-gun close at hand. In spite of what he said, there was a report that two of the worst of the supervisors had escaped, and it was not certain where they were or if they had any firearms. O'Grady would be ready just in case.

Cormac stood a dozen yards away. Canyon would hear anything that moved within fifty yards. He settled down, watched the even breathing of the beautiful little lady in his arms, and went to sleep.

An angry blue jay awoke him just at dawn. Three large beasts were in the middle of the blue jay's territory and he let them know about it. Canyon looked around before he moved, saw nothing out of the ordinary, and then glanced down at Melissa. She had one hand over his chest. She slept on her side and had a wonderful smile showing.

He bent and kissed her cheek. She mumbled something in her sleep. He lifted away from her and started the fire, then fed Cormac two handsful of oats and moved him to a spot of fresh grass.

Melissa awoke, sat up, and stretched as graceful as

a spring fawn. She looked around, saw Canyon, and smiled.

"Good, wonderful, marvelous, outstanding morning, Canyon O'Grady." She jumped to her feet, ran to him, kissed him, and then hugged him. Her face then took on a veil of seriousness. "I've decided. I can't stay here in the valley. There are too many bad memories. I want to go to my aunt's family. They live in Omaha."

He hugged her and let her go. "Good, I think that's the best plan for you. We can get you a stage in Denver. I want to take a look at the town anyway while I'm so close. There is a telegraph there, I think. We'll find out."

"So, let's ride back to the village and have some breakfast at the community kitchen," Melissa said. "I'm sure it'll be open again. Then I'll pack what I'll need. Most of the clothes I'll leave for the women in the village."

They cleaned up their camp, made sure the fire was out, and rode back to the village. As they came toward it, they saw men in the fields. A wagon of men was headed toward the gold mine. But the men seemed to have a different attitude. Now they were working because they wanted to and at jobs they had some interest in.

The village seemed normal. Shops and stores were open. People moved around the streets. At the village bulletin board there was a notice in large printing.

"Nominating petitions now being accepted for positions of mayor, and six councilmen. Pick up instructions at the Village Hall (formerly the palace)."

Other notices were up. One wanted a seamstress. One was a farmer looking for work. Another asked about drivers to take the three stagecoaches back to Denver, where they belonged.

Canyon and Melissa went to the communal kitchen, where O'Grady had eaten a meal once, and found breakfast being served. The manager stood at the head of the line.

"We know not many of you have any money yet, but for those who do, we'd appreciate some help in financing. We'll be a restaurant soon. Everything in town will be on a commercial basis."

O'Grady searched his purse and found a gold coin worth $2.50. He put it in the man's box. "For two breakfasts and a dinner I had here before," Canyon said.

"That's too much," the manager said.

"I'll get it back on my expense tally," the agent said, chuckling, and they went through the breakfast line.

They were half-finished with the meal when Elder Teincuff came over to the table where they sat.

"Mr. O'Grady, Miss Klingman, I'm glad I found you. We have a former lawyer who wants to be our district attorney, even though we don't have a district yet. Mr. O'Grady, the man wants to know if you wish to file any charges against anyone for stealing the U.S. mail, you being a representative of the government."

"No. It wouldn't hold up in a regular court anyway, Elder Teincuff. But thanks for asking. I'd like to be one of the drivers for a stage going out. What time will they be leaving the village?"

"About noon, near as I can tell," Teincuff said. "We have ten people who want to ride out. Some will go to Fort Collins, some to Denver. Oh, we searched and found those three bags of mail on the stages. It'll be a little late, but now it can get through."

"I'll check at the stables for the coaches," O'Grady said.

Elder Teincuff sat down and wiped his forehead. "It's been a busy morning already."

"Things look more like they did two years ago," Melissa put in.

"Yes, starting to," Teincuff said. "We have so much

to do. We've decided to call this Hidden Valley Village, and Hidden Valley County when the territory gets organized. We'll use the former palace as the Village Hall and government building. We'll be sending a man out to Denver asking for a branch bank to be established here and to set up a United States post office as well.

"We can produce more than we need in the valley, so we'll have goods to sell: beef, wheat, corn, and hogs. It will take us a year or so to convert from a commune type of economy, but we'll take care of our own here. Nobody will go hungry or cold in Hidden Valley Village."

"Sounds like you're running for mayor already, Teincuff," O'Grady said.

"I'm filing for it. We'll see."

When breakfast was over, they went to Melissa's former room at the castle. Everyone smiled and waved at her. No animosity was held against her. Nothing had been touched in her room. She took only a few of the more durable and common clothes. The grand gowns she left for the town.

"I have no jewels, Daddy didn't think that way. So all I can leave the town are the dresses he had made." She packed a leather suitcase.

Canyon left her to her task and went to the livery. They needed another driver, and he signed on. The coaches were being checked out, the axles regreased, the running gear inspected, and the seats inside wiped down and scrubbed clean. The rigs were ready to roll.

There were three coaches, which meant twelve horses. The livery manager hated to let them go, but he realized the twelve had been stolen from the stage company and had to be replaced.

O'Grady inspected the animals selected and rejected two of them. The stable man grinned. He was trying some old-fashioned horse trading, but he didn't get away with it.

The horses were harnessed up and the rigs were ready. They drove them to the Village Hall and waited for the passengers. Each person was instructed to bring along enough food for themselves for four days. It would take at least that long to get to Denver, since they would have no regular relay stations.

One of the rigs would go to Fort Collins and two turn the other way to Denver.

Canyon saw Melissa coming down the Village Hall steps, and two young men rushed up to help her carry her suitcase to the coach. O'Grady waved at her, and one of the young men hoisted her bag to the rack on top, where Canyon secured it down with some other luggage.

Melissa wore a sturdy blue skirt with trousers underneath. She had a hat with a wide brim and a tie-down strap under her chin. She motioned for Canyon to help her and stepped to the top seat beside the driver. "I'm riding shotgun for you," Melissa said, and grinned.

"No shotgun," he said.

Just then someone came out of the Village Hall with a shotgun for each of the coaches. The rigs arrived with a shotgun each. They should return that way, the man who handed up the weapon said.

Melissa touched Canyon's sleeve. "I know it won't be as fine as last night," she said softly so no one else could hear. "But whatever it is, we'll be together for three or four more days. I'll settle for that. I know you have your job and must go back to Washington. But I have my memories. Things will be fine for me in Omaha."

O'Grady patted her shoulder and straightened the eight strands of leather reins in his two gloved hands. Melissa would be fine. They would find time and place to make love again during the next three nights.

Canyon thought about Ella and the time he had spent with her. With the fervor of the last twenty-four hours he hadn't even had a chance to say good-bye. But he knew that a girl that adventurous would have little trouble finding a man in the new village of Hidden Valley.

He looked around and grinned. Never in his short Irishman's days had he figured he'd have this much adventure, this kind of an exciting life. He had long ago decided that nothing could be better.

He got the signal from the other drivers and slapped the reins down on the backs of the four horses.

"Hiiiiiiyaaaaaa! Let's move out them critters. We've got to get this young lady to Denver city."

Melissa squeezed his arm as dust shot up around the wagon wheels and they were off. . . .

KEEP A LOOKOUT!

The following is the opening section from the next novel in the action-packed new Signet Western series CANYON O'GRADY

CANYON O'GRADY #8

BLEEDING KANSAS

Buckeye Springs, Kansas, August 12, 1858.
New Territories Kansas and Nebraska are up for grabs
whether to be free or slave states. Both sides
pour in settlers for the vote of the people to decide.
Emotions run high, violence is rampant
—Kansas is bleeding. . . .

Canyon O'Grady neared the town late in the afternoon. He passed a burned-out farm about two miles outside of the settlement. A man stood there looking at his half-ruined barn and a house that was nothing but ashes and a brick chimney.

There was no smoke and the ashes appeared to be cold. The night riders must have been at their dirty business again. O'Grady hoped that he could ride a tight line between the two factions. The "civil war" between the slavery and antislavery parties had been roaring here for three years. John Brown had done his dirty deeds and left the state. Men on both sides had been killed. The Kansas militia had been called out, and federal troops from various forts had been used to help defuse the open warfare that flared from time to time.

O'Grady's reading of the current position was that the southern cause had been much the stronger in the early days of the conflict, but that now new power and emigrants from the North had edged the tide of the battle toward the antislavery faction.

He was going to do his best to investigate the murder of U.S. Marshal J. B. Tippit and try to steer clear of everything else. At least, that was his fondest hope. He knew the slavery question was one absolutely loaded with emotion. Normally rational men and women went crazy when it came up, and that usually led to violence.

O'Grady rode Cormac down the main street of the town and saw where a business had been burned to the ground. There was no new construction going on here as he had seen in much of the West. It was said that no thinking man would bring a wife and family into the hotbed of violence that Kansas had become.

Still, new families of the southern persuasion did come across the border from Missouri. Those coming into the territory favoring the North and antislavery had to skirt to the north of Missouri and come through Iowa and Nebraska. This route was the only one possible if a northern sympathizer wanted to bring in any weapons.

O'Grady found that Meg Ryson had been right: Buckeye Springs had only one hotel, a two-story affair almost in the middle of the small town. He guessed there were no more than five hundred people in the settlement, but many more than that in outlying sections, where some farming was starting and cattle were being raised.

The special agent for the President of the United States tied up outside the hotel, unslung the carpetbag off the back of Cormac, and went in to register.

His room on the second floor was about what he expected—stark, clean, and almost bare. A bed, a dresser with a mirror, a pitcher of water and a bowl, and one chair were its only comforts. He dropped his carpetbag on the bed and went to put Cormac in the livery stable.

The stable was smaller than he had figured. Not many travelers passed through Buckeye Springs, and most of the people kept their own horses in town or on the farms and ranches.

For twenty cents a day he got a stall and some hay, but he had to furnish his own grain. He paid another nickel a day for oats and unsaddled the big palomino and brushed him down. The stallion turned and nuzzled O'Grady and rolled his big brown eyes, but there was no apple in his owner's pocket this time.

"Next time, lad," O'Grady said. "Next time it'll be an apple and sugar." On his way back to the hotel, he passed the small, wood-framed Ashland County courthouse. A sign over a side door said, SHERIFF'S DEPARTMENT.

O'Grady hesitated. He didn't know who to trust in this town, not with the slavery fight. He'd heard that in one east Kansas county the sheriff, judges, and the district attorney all lined up on one side of the slavery issue and wouldn't prosecute any crimes, including murders and arson, committed by men working for their side.

First he'd look around and do some careful questioning. After it got dark he would go see the woman who wrote the first letter to the U.S. marshal's office, Tabitha Rothmore. He might try the back door of the general store just before she closed up.

O'Grady was almost back to the hotel when he saw someone riding into town. The man sat hunched over in the saddle, favoring his right shoulder. The horse moved at a slow walk, and with each step of the mount, the rider winced. He angled toward the side of the street where O'Grady stood. When the horse came to the tie rail, it stopped. The man looked at the building in front of him. O'Grady did, too, and saw that it was a doctor's office.

The rider slipped halfway out of the saddle.

O'Grady rushed out and caught him, saw the blood on his shoulder, and eased him down from the mount. The big Irishman put the rider's good arm over his shoulder and his arm around the man's waist and almost carried him to the boardwalk and up to the doctor's door.

"Figure you want to see the doc," O'Grady said.

"Right," the man said through tightly held lips.

Inside the doctor's office, they found a woman in a white dress who saw the blood and hurried them through the waiting area to a small room with a chair and a waist-high table. O'Grady helped the man onto the table and pushed a small pillow under his head.

A few seconds later a short, thin man with deep-set eyes and hair cut short in the Prussian style hurried into the room.

"Blinman!" The little medico shook his head. "Told you that was fire you was playing with. Told you it was gonna burn you sooner or later. Hell! The issue is nearly settled. Let it lay."

He used some scissors to cut off a patch of the man's shirt and examined the wound.

"They didn't figure to miss, did they? You got powder burns on your shirt and skin around that bullet hole. How far away was the bastard?"

"About three feet, Doc. Can you get the slug out?"

"Sure. How loud can you scream?"

"Loud enough. Start digging. Damn thing's been in there since last night."

"Want your friend to help hold you down?" the doctor asked.

"Don't know the gent." Blinman looked up. "Thanks, stranger. I might still be lying out there in the dust if you hadn't helped. This ain't exactly a friendly town, not anymore."

O'Grady touched his hat and walked out of the room and the office. He stopped by at the first saloon he saw, the Hell Hole. O'Grady snorted. Probably a well-founded name. But the best saloon in a community usually is the quickest place to find out what's going on in town. He pushed inside, bought a beer for a dime at the bar, and settled down at the end of the polished wood to listen and wash down the trail dust at the same time.

Five minutes later a man who dressed like a clerk in a store came in and looked behind him. He asked for a beer and then talked to the apron.

"You hear that Blinman got himself shot? Last night sometime. Them night riders burned him out slicker than a whistle. Shot him on purpose from what I hear. Punishment. A damned clear warning."

"Which side he on?" the barkeep asked.

"Damned if I know. But if he got a pistol shot up close that way, he must have been a northerner. I hear the southern night riders burn and then shoot the victim that way as a lesson."

"I don't take sides," the barkeep said, holding up both hands. "Hell, I want to stay alive. I just don't take sides."

"Not that much going on anymore, Amos. You should have been here three years ago. Damn, it was hell on wheels around here in fifty-five and fifty-six. Calmed down ever so much since them wild years."

"Still, we had that hanging about two months ago."

The clerk sipped his beer, then scratched his head. "Ain't nobody thinks that had much to do with the slavery question. Far as anybody can tell, that is. That killing certainly was an interesting one."

The clerk finished his beer, nodded at the apron, and headed out the front door.

O'Grady followed him. It was getting on toward dusk. He walked the town, one end to the other, covering both sides of the street. Not a lot of town to look over. He found the general store and saw that it had the CLOSED sign out. He went to the alley and up to the back door of the store and knocked. He knocked a second and then a third time.

"Yes, who is it?" a muffled voice came from inside.

"I'm new in town, miss. I need to talk with you."

"I'm closed, go away."

"Can't do that. I want to talk about your father."

He heard a bolt thrown, then the door edged open an inch. It was light inside.

"You said you want to talk about my father. What about?"

"I'm trying to find out who killed him."

The door came open more and he saw her. She was tiny, maybe five feet tall and eighty-five pounds wet. She had light-blond hair to her shoulders with straight bangs in front. In the lamplight he could see a strong chin and high cheekbones. She was a pretty girl—not a beauty, but pretty.

Canyon had a first impression that this girl was strong-willed and still angry.

She stared at him from soft green eyes. "I don't see no badge. Who are you?"

"My name is Canyon O'Grady and I'm interested in your father's death and the death of the U.S. marshal who came here at the urging of your letters."

"Oh. If you know about them, then you must be a lawman. I guess it's all right to let you come in." She held open the door.

Just then a gunshot sounded behind them and a round thunked into the wood over the door.

"Don't neither of you move a tad or you're dead. Understand?" a soft southern voice called out before the sound of the shot could die out.

O'Grady froze, his hand starting down his right side. "Yes, I understand."

"Good. You, big man, move to the side and stretch your hands to the top of the door. Do it slow. I don't aim to kill nobody. Just want to relieve the little lady of her cash. She took in a basket of money today. I been watching."

The voice was still well behind them.

"Little lady, you just best unbutton your blouse there and show me what you're hiding underneath. Yeah, good idea. Do it right now."

"No!"

"What the hell you say? I got a gun."

O'Grady could see just the edge of the girl where she stood in the door. A fraction of a second later she darted to one side and was gone. The light inside blew out and the gunman roared in anger and stormed toward the door.

O'Grady timed it by the sound of the man's angry breathing. Just as he came beside the tall agent, O'Grady slammed his fist downward into the gunman's way. His fist hit the robber's right wrist, spinning his iron out of his hand. O'Grady whirled and kicked the man's legs out from under him, sprawling the man in the dust.

A split second later O'Grady pushed his big six-gun under the robber's chin and pressed upward so hard it made the man cry out in pain.

"The fight is gone out of him, Miss Rothmore," O'Grady said. "Our friend is ready to apologize and swear that he's heading out of town right now."

A light bloomed in the back room of the general

store and Tabitha Rothmore carried it forward, a shotgun now under one arm. O'Grady saw that both hammers were cocked on the double barrels.

She stood looking down at the gunman lying in the dust by the back door of the general store.

"Know him?" O'Grady asked.

"Never seen him before . . . No, I have. I sold him a box of percussion caps and linen-wrapped cartridges for a forty-four-caliber six-gun this afternoon."

"Want me to call the sheriff?" O'Grady asked.

"Wouldn't do much good. We haven't had a trial here in the county for almost two years. Our judge quit. The district attorney was shot dead, and the sheriff is more worried about his job and his outside interests than he is in law and order."

"Stand up," O'Grady ordered the robber. The man stood slowly, O'Grady's .44 army percussion Colt never leaving his chin. "You have any money?" O'Grady asked.

"Three dollars," the man said.

"You better use that to get yourself as far out of town as you can. I'm gonna be around for a couple of weeks. I see your face anywhere, I'm gonna blow it full of extra holes. You understand?"

"Yes sir. Do I get my six-gun back?"

"Not a chance," Tabitha said quickly. "I'm making a collection of guns men have used to try to rob me. So far I've got two. Now I'll have one more. Just for your information, nobody has robbed me yet. I've got one scalp on my scalp pole, courtesy of my trusty shotgun. You want to try again?"

The man shook his head.

O'Grady prodded him in the belly with the six-gun. "Get out of here," he said. "All the way out of the county. Out of the territory would be safest for you."

The man turned and stared at them a minute in the light.

Excerpt from *BLEEDING KANSAS*

O'Grady put a hot lead slug into the ground between his boots, and the man raced down the alley into the darkness. Canyon holstered his iron and tipped his hat.

"Now, Miss Rothmore, I need to have a confidential talk with you about your father's death and just what the U.S. marshal said and did while he was here."

Tabitha Rothmore let a small smile creep onto her pretty face. "So, I figured you had to be some kind of lawman. Nobody else has been interested in that marshal. Come in and we'll shut the door. That owlhoot might just have a second iron in his saddlebag down the alley . . ."

LIFE ON THE FRONTIER

☐ **THE OCTOPUS by Frank Norris.** Rippling miles of grain in the San Joaquin Valley in California are the prize in a titanic struggle between the powerful farmers who grow the wheat and the railroad monopoly that controls its transportation. As the struggle flourishes it yields a grim harvest of death and disillusion, financial and moral ruin. "One of the few American novels to bring a significant episode from our history to life."—Robert Spiller (524527—$4.95)

☐ **THE OUTCASTS OF POKER FLAT and Other Tales by Bret Harte.** Stories of 19th century Far West and the glorious fringe-inhabitants of Gold Rush California. Introduction by Wallace Stegner, Stanford University. (523466—$4.50)

☐ **THE CALL OF THE WILD and Selected Stories by Jack London.** Foreword by Franklin Walker. The American author's vivid picture of the wild life of a dog and a man in the Alaska gold fields. (523903—$2.50)

☐ **LAUGHING BOY by Oliver LaFarge.** The greatest novel yet written about the American Indian, this Pulitzer-prize winner has not been available in paperback for many years. It is, quite simply, the love story of Laughing Boy and Slim Girl—a beautifully written, poignant, moving account of an Indian marriage. (522443—$3.50)

☐ **THE DEERSLAYER by James Fenimore Cooper.** The classic frontier saga of an idealistic youth, raised among the Indians, who emerges to face life with a nobility as pure and proud as the wilderness whose fierce beauty and freedom have claimed his heart. (516451—$2.95)

☐ **THE OX-BOW INCIDENT by Walter Van Tilburg Clark.** A relentlessly honest novel of violence and quick justice in the Old West. Afterword by Walter Prescott Webb. (523865—$3.95)

Prices slightly higher in Canada.

Buy them at your local

bookstore or use coupon

on next page for ordering.